THE BANANA SPLIT AFFAIR

Cynthia Blair

FAWCETT JUNIPER • NEW YORK

RLI: $\dfrac{\text{VL: 5 \& up}}{\text{IL: 6 \& up}}$

A Fawcett Juniper Book
Published by Ballantine Books

Library of Congress Catalog Card Number: 84-90954

ISBN 0-449-70175-1

Manufactured in the United States of America

First Edition: February 1985
Eleventh Printing: June 1988

One

"Thomas J. Turner! Why on earth *should I let you kiss* me? Every girl in the junior class knows what a flirt you are!"

The sound of Christine Pratt's gay voice floated up to the second floor windows of her family's house. It was followed by the slam of a car door and light footsteps hurrying up the front walk.

Susan, her twin, abandoned her watercolor paints and rushed over to the bedroom window. She was just in time to see her sister, Chris, flounce up the walk with a confident toss of her head. Her cheeks were flushed and her eyes sparkled.

"I'm not even sure I'll agree to go out with you the next time you phone me!" Chris called to her date with a playful grin before disappearing into the house.

Susan could only imagine Tommy Turner's response as he drove away. Boys seemed to love it when Chris teased them. They were always coming back for more. The telephone at the Pratts' rang constantly, and there was a steady stream of junior and senior boys lining up outside the house in their cars.

And all that male attention was always for Chris. Never for Susan. Most of the boys weren't even aware that the vivacious, popular Christine Pratt had an identical twin sister.

Indentical twin sisters. When the two Pratts stood side by side, it was almost impossible to tell that they were both versions of the same sixteen-year-old girl. Susan turned to face the mirror that hung over her dresser.

"Identical!" she said aloud, her voice scornful. "Hah!"

"Did you say something?" Her mother poked her head in the doorway of Susan's bedroom. "Or have you started talking to yourself? Don't tell me one of my sixteen-year-old daughters is already becoming senile!"

Susan glanced over at her mother and smiled sheepishly.

"Actually, I was talking to the mirror," she confessed.

"That sounds interesting." Mrs. Pratt came into the room and sat down on the edge of the bed. She had been wiling away the leisurely October Sunday afternoon with a mystery novel, one of her favorite ways of relaxing after a long week of hard work. As she sat down, she folded over the edge of the page she had been reading and closed the book, preparing for a heart-to-heart talk with her daughter. "Is the mirror talking back to you?"

"Yes, it is, as a matter of fact."

"What does it have to say?"

Susan sighed woefully. "It says that Christine and I are the two most unlikely girls in the world to have been born twins."

"Why is that?" Her mother looked puzzled, as well as concerned. "You and Chris have a great deal in common. You're both bright and pretty and interested in a lot of things. . . ."

"But, Mother!" Susan wailed. "Just *look* at us! We look like Beauty and the Beast!"

"Susan, that's not true!" her mother said sharply. "You seem to be forgetting one very simple fact. You and Chris are *identical* twins. You have the exact same faces! So how could either of you be prettier than the other?"

Susan knew that her mother was right. The twins did have the same features: high cheekbones, delicate coloring, cute ski-jump noses. They shared the same dark brown eyes and chestnut hair. Even their tall slender figures were similar.

What was so different about them was the way they used their physical characteristics to express their personalities. Staring at her reflection, Susan decided that her looks were as plain as the quiet, bookish girl to whom they belonged. Her shoulder-length hair was always worn the same way, parted in the middle, hanging straight down. She rarely bothered to wear any makeup: A freshly scrubbed look was good enough for her. Her clothes were always neat and clean, but they bordered on drab. Pale colors, simple styles, small prints. Susan Pratt was basically a pretty girl, but it was as if she were doing her best to hide that fact from the rest of the world.

Chris, on the other hand, spent hours and hours on her appearance. She *wanted* to be noticed. It was true in the way she acted: outgoing, self-confident, sometimes even arrogant. And it was equally true in the way she looked.

She carefully applied mascara, blush, and lip gloss before leaving the house, even if she were just going to the corner store to pick up a fashion magazine.

"You never know who you might run into," she would say.

Chris's dresser was cluttered with the face creams and shampoos and special soaps she was constantly experimenting with. Her hair, parted on the side, was always held off her face with pretty combs or barrettes that matched her outfit, and she often wore it in tight braids overnight to give it soft waves during the day. While most of Susan's allowance and baby-sitting money was saved up for books and art supplies, Chris's went to stylish blouses or bright-colored tee shirts to go with the fitted jeans she liked to wear.

"If Chris and I are so much the same," Susan pouted, still gazing at her reflection, "then why is it that she spent this afternoon going to the movies with one of her millions of boyfriends, while I stayed alone in my room, painting?"

"You're just a late bloomer, that's all." Her mother rose from the bed and gave her daughter a sympathetic hug. "People develop at different rates. Don't forget, you've just turned sixteen. I'll bet the boys will start hanging around you any day now.

"Besides, what about your artwork? You're a very talented painter. Surely that must give you a lot of satisfaction. I bet Chris would give anything to be able to paint like that." She motioned toward the sensitive watercolor of a beach scene in soft blues and greens, nearly completed, that sat on the desk.

"I doubt it," Susan mumbled. "What good is being able to paint compared to having every boy at school dying to go out with you?"

Mrs. Pratt chuckled. "I think that's an exaggeration. Chris herself would probably laugh if she heard you say that. She does have a lot of dates, but she's hardly the social butterfly you seem to think she is. Besides, I doubt that she really cares very much about any of the boys she goes out with."

From downstairs in the kitchen came the sounds of Chris turning on the radio and singing along with a popular song as she made herself a snack.

"I'd better go down now and make sure Chris doesn't make a total shambles of the kitchen. In the meantime, why don't you give some thought to what you've been mooning about? Nobody's life is perfect. Certainly not Christine's. You're a very lucky girl, Susan. You've got an awful lot going for you. I just wish you could see that for yourself."

As her mother started downstairs, Susan shook her head slowly and turned away from the mirror. She went back to her desk and the watercolor she had been working on all afternoon. As much as she tried to concentrate on mixing just the right shade of blue for the sky, she couldn't stop thinking about her sister.

Susan would gladly have traded her straight-A average, even her outstanding artistic talent, for some of her twin's flair with people—especially boys. If only she were bubbly enough to attract someone like . . . well, someone like Keith West, the quiet blond-haired boy in her art class. But he was so shy that it would take a lot to get him to ask her out. It would take more courage than the bashful Susan Pratt could ever hope to muster up. So as far as she was concerned, the situation with Keith was hopeless.

I'll never be like Chris, she thought sadly. It's not even worth daydreaming about, since I'll never get to experience life the way she does. We're as different as night and day.

It had been that way for as long as Susan could

remember. Even when they were little girls, Chris was the outgoing one. Whenever their parents' friends came over, she was only too happy to sing and play the piano and charm strangers. Susan, on the other hand, would hide in the kitchen for as long as she could, terrified of meeting those same people. Once she was forced to come out to meet the guests, she would stand before them shyly, red-faced and so nervous that she couldn't think of a single thing to say.

"How different your twins are!" people would exclaim to their mother. "Christine is so friendly, and as loveable as a puppy. But Susan is so quiet. . . ."

"She'll grow out of it," Mrs. Pratt would assure them quickly. "Besides, she's the smart one. Her father and I expect her to grow up to be a doctor or a scientist. Susan could read by the time she was four years old."

Susan always felt as if her mother were making excuses for her. But it was true that she was brighter than her sister, so she worked hard to maintain the A average that differentiated her from her outgoing, popular twin. Besides, studying and doing well in school were much easier for her than forcing herself to overcome her shyness and talk to people.

So their roles were established almost as soon as the twins could talk. Chris was the personable one, the one who loved to chatter away and be the center of attention and make friends. Susan was the quiet one who was expected to do well at her studies and eventually become something important.

With a heavy heart, Susan returned to her watercolor, frowning as she tried to decide which colors to mix together to get just the right shade for the sky. Following her mother's advice, she thought about all her good points as she watched the glass of water turn darker and cloudier as she cleaned her brush in it. She mentally listed all the positive qualities that Susan Pratt, Christine Pratt's shy sister who did her best to fade into the wallpaper wherever she went, possessed.

But a few seconds later she heard her sister bound up the stairs. Chris would be anxious to share all the details of her Sunday-afternoon date with Tommy Turner, Susan knew. As usual, she would breathlessly report on where they had gone, what he had said, how she had flirted with him.

For now Susan's painting would have to wait. Her shoulders drooped as she dropped her brush into the water. She was in no mood to hear Chris giggle and brag as she told her twin all about her latest escapade. But it was hardly the first time she had felt that way. And so she gritted her teeth and forced herself to smile.

TWO

Christine Pratt stood in front of the open refrigerator and frowned. She was trying to decide what to have for a snack. She was starving after spending the afternoon out, running around with Tommy Turner. She hadn't had anything to eat since popcorn at the movies, and that had been hours earlier.

"Let's see," she mumbled, switching on the radio loudly and singing along with it. "I would *kill* for some of that apple pie left over from last night's dinner. But if I keep eating at this rate, I'll never manage to fit into my jeans."

Chris dutifully reached past the pie and took an apple out of the bowl behind it. A piece of fruit was hardly the same thing as apple pie, but as long as looking good was her highest priority, it would have to do.

"Don't eat too much," she heard her mother's voice warn. "Dinner will be ready in an hour or so."

Chis whirled around to see her mother standing in the

8

doorway of the kitchen. "Oh, hi, Mom. What's for dinner?"

"Chicken."

"Yum. My favorite. And if we're not eating for an hour, I have time to wash my hair before then."

"Chris, how about going up to your sister's room instead? She could probably use some company. She spent the whole day in her room painting. Besides, I think she needs some cheering up."

"Sooz needs cheering up? How come?" Chris perched on a high wooden stool and bit into her apple. With a gesture that had become second nature to her, she reached up and smoothed her hair, making sure it was in place.

"She's feeling a bit blue."

A look of concern crossed Chris's face. "Really? Nothing serious, I hope."

"No, nothing serious. But I think a twin-to-twin talk might be in order."

"Okay." Chris took another bite of her apple and hopped off her stool. "I'll tell you what. I'll even bring her an apple as a goodwill gesture. She's probably dying of hunger after being holed up in her room all alone for hours on end."

"Chris!"

"What?" Chris asked innocently, retrieving a second apple from the refrigerator. "What did I say?"

"You make it sound as if there were something wrong with spending time alone."

"There's nothing *wrong* with it." She shrugged. "I've just never been very good at it." She paused and chewed a bite of apple.

"Come to think of it, that's probably why I never did very well in school. And why I was never good at anything in particular, the way Susan is. Like art, I mean. I just don't have the self-discipline. I'm too busy running all over the place like a chicken with its head cut off."

She thought for a minute, then added in an unusually pensive tone, "It's too bad I'm that way. I'll never be able to accomplish anything worthwhile. I guess I'm just not as lucky as Susan."

Mrs. Pratt's mouth dropped open. She was astounded by Chris's comment. But before she could say a word, her daughter had skipped out of the kitchen and was headed for the stairs.

She ran up them energetically, two at a time. Breathlessly, she waltzed into her twin's bedroom.

"Hiya, Sooz. Here, I brought you an apple. I want to be remembered as someone who helped cultivate a great talent. If I can't be a famous artist, at least I can help *you* get there. Maybe you'll even dedicate a painting to me someday. Or do my portrait. I can see it now: *Girl in Blue Jeans*. Or better yet: *Girl with Frizzy Hair*."

"Hi, Chris. Thanks for the apple. I'm famished."

Chris glanced around her sister's bedroom. Hung all along every wall were paintings and drawings done by Susan. And each one was more impressive than the last. Portraits, landscapes, still lifes—Susan seemed to have a knack for them all. And she had used every medium imaginable, from crayons and colored pencils to oil paints and paper collages.

As she noticed the seascape on the desk, she felt a twinge of regret. While she had spent her Sunday afternoon flirting with a boy she didn't even particularly *like*, her twin had used the time to create a beautiful painting she would have forever.

Not that *I could*, Chris thought sadly, even if I tried.

The next thing that caught her eye as her sister swiveled around in her chair so they could talk were the shelves and shelves of books. Some of the titles sounded interesting, some of them just plain dull. But she knew that Susan had read them all. Not only that; she had probably also *learned* something from each one. Chris never managed to find much time to read. She was too busy talking on the telephone and braiding her hair and going out on dates.

Susan probably *will* become someone important one day, she thought, suddenly feeling sorry for herself. Maybe even someone *great*.

"So tell me, Chris," Susan was saying to her as she plopped down on the bed. "How was you date with Tommy Turner?"

"It was okay," she answered distractedly.

"What did you do?"

"Oh, nothing much."

"Where did you go?"

"A movie."

"Are you going out with him again sometime?"

"I don't know." Chris sounded as if her thoughts were a thousand miles away.

Susan finally said impatiently, "For heaven's sake, Chris, what's the matter with you? I thought you *liked* Tommy. I mean you *are* going out with him!"

"He's okay."

"Then what's wrong? Or is it that you don't want to tell me about it?"

"Oh, Sooz, it has nothing to do with you. The truth is it was a total waste of an afternoon. I had a terrible time. I should never have gone out today, with Tommy Turner or anyone else. I was so worried about that history test tomorrow that I couldn't think about anything else."

She stood up and began pacing around the room. "I couldn't concentrate on Tommy or the movie or anything. I kept seeing little dates dancing before my eyes— 1492, 1812. . . ."

"That's too bad," Susan clucked, still envious that her sister had at least *had* the option of going out on a date.

"Hey, Chris, that's a pretty scarf." Susan eyed the red wool muffler thrown carelessly around her sister's neck. "I don't think I've ever seen it before. Is it new?"

"Not exactly. It was Tommy's. He gave it to me just now. He said it made my eyes gleam like an Arabian princess's." Chris sounded bored. She paused near the desk and gave Susan's watercolor an admiring glance. "That's terrific, Sooz! I love the color of the ocean. It looks so real! It reminds me of the time we went to the shore with Mom and Dad last summer."

"Thanks." Despite her sister's sudden enthusiasm, Susan still sensed that something was wrong. She hesitantly asked, "Is everything all right, Chris? You seem kind of down. Did anything happen with Tommy?"

"Something *is* wrong, but it has nothing to do with Tommy." Chris dropped onto the bed once again. She sighed deeply, then said, "Gee, Susan. I'm so envious of you! Look at that painting you did this afternoon. You whipped it off like it was nothing. I wish I could paint like that. Look at this room. It reminds me of an art museum!

"And I wish I could get A's as easily as you can. Except for math, I never do very well in school. I'm going to have to spend the whole night studying for that stupid history test, and I'll bet anything that I'll *still* end up getting a C and a lecture from Mr. Stevens. He's always saying, 'Christine, why can't you be more like your twin? She gets A's without even trying!' Everything comes so easily to you." She pulled off the scarf and tossed it onto the bed beside her. "Oh, Susan," she cried, "sometimes I wish I were you!"

Susan was so flabbergasted that she nearly dropped her brush and ruined her painting. "Chris, I can't believe you just said that! Maybe there really *is* something to the idea of twins being on the same wavelength! Unless you happen to be some kind of mind reader."

"What do you mean, Sooz? Did I miss something?" Chris looked puzzled.

"I was just sitting here watching you from my window and wishing that *I* were *you*!"

"You're kidding!" Chris squealed. "You wish you were *me*? Whatever for?"

"Mainly because you're all the things that I'm not! You're popular with boys. You always know the right thing to say. You always look like you just stepped off a page of *Seventeen* magazine. . . ."

"But Sooz! You're positively *brilliant*! All the teachers love you. You hardly have to put in any time studying. Plus you happen to be an artistic *genius*. . . . How could I *not* wish I were more like you?"

Susan stared off into space thoughtfully. "I guess it *is* kind of funny that even though we're identical twins, we turned out to be so different. We're practically the exact opposites of each other. We couldn't be less alike if we tried." She paused for a few seconds, then chuckled to herself.

"What are you laughing at?"

"Oh, nothing. I just had a crazy idea, that's all."

"What?"

"It's silly." Susan dismissed her thought with a wave of her hand.

"Come on. Try me," Chris insisted. "I promise I won't laugh."

"Well, here I am, wishing I were you. And here you are, wishing you were me. It's really too bad. What we need is a fairy godmother who could take all our personality traits and combine them and split them between us equally. Then we wouldn't have to go around wishing we were each other."

"Yeah," Chris sighed. "Too bad there's no such thing as magic. I'd give anything to find out what it's like to be you, even for just a few days."

"I know," Susan agreed. "I'd love to find out what it's like to be you, too. Wouldn't it be wonderful if we could really change places for a while?"

The two girls were silent for a minute, each lost in her own thoughts. And then, suddenly, a devilish look came into Chris's eyes. At the same time, a similar expression crept over Susan's face. The twins looked across the room at each other.

"Sooz," Chris said softly, "are you by any chance thinking what I'm thinking?"

"Yes," said Susan in the same tone.

Diabolical grins appeared on both girls' faces.

"*We could trade lives!*" Susan's voice was barely more than a whisper. "I mean we could trade identities!"

"Yes! Oh, yes!" Chris clapped her hands. "I could become you, and you could become me! After all, we're identical twins. We could make ourselves look like each other!"

"We could dress like each other. . . ."

"And act like each other . . ."

"And no one would be able to tell the difference!"

"That's right!" cried Chris. "I'd get to be Susan Pratt, and you'd get to be Christine Pratt!"

The two girls broke into peals of hysterical laughter at the idea of changing lives and identities with each other. It was a wonderful fantasy, one that was so obvious that neither could believe it had never occurred to them before.

"So when do we start?" Chris asked when the two of them had quieted down and caught their breath. "How about tonight?"

"What?" Susan gasped. "Do you really mean it? You'd actually go through with something like that?"

"Of course! Why not? You were just saying you wanted to be me. And I'd jump at the chance to try being you. So let's do it!"

"We can't just become each other," Susan protested. "It's crazy!"

"So much the better. Sooz, we *have* to do it, now that we've thought of it. It's too good an idea to pass up!"

"Do you think we could really fool people?"

"You bet! As a matter of fact, I'll bet you the biggest banana split you can find that no one will guess that we've switched identities."

Susan tried to think up some reason why switching lives with her twin for a while would never work. Eventually she had to admit that there were few good reasons not to give it a try. Meanwhile, Chris watched her anxiously, eager to hear her decision.

Finally she took a deep breath and said, "Okay, Chris. It's a deal. But the banana split bet is still on. If we manage to carry this thing off, I'll buy you one. And if we get found out, you do the buying."

"You're on!" Chris threw her arms around her twin. "What an absolute brainstorm! Oooh, I can't wait to get started!"

Susan suddenly drew away and frowned. "Hold on a minute, Chris. We won't switch *forever*, will we?"

"Of course not. That would be impossible, even if we wanted to. No, all we want is a chance to experience life the way the other twin does. That's the whole reason for this, isn't it? We'll do it for . . . Let's see. . . . How about two weeks?"

"Hmmm. Today is Sunday, so that'll be two full weeks of school and two weekends. Sounds fair. Not too long, but we'll still have a chance to get a taste of each other's lives. Okay. I'm game!"

"Terrific! I knew you'd come through, Sooz!"

In her usual organized manner, Susan took out a piece of paper and a pen. "All right. So it's agreed. Now we'll have to work out the details of our plan."

"What details?" Chris asked impatiently, gleefully throwing the red scarf up into the air.

"For one thing, we've got to decide who we'll tell. *Somebody* has to know what's going on."

Chris crossed her legs Indian-style and rested her chin in her hands. "Let's not tell anybody. Not a living soul." Her brown eyes gleamed mischievously.

Susan shook her head. "No, we'll have to tell someone. In case something goes wrong."

"What could possibly go wrong?" Chris pouted. But when she noticed her sister's stern expression, she said, "Oh, all right. I suppose you've got a point. As usual. You're always so levelheaded. Who do you think we should tell?"

"We should at least tell Mom and Dad."

"Okay," Chris agreed. "We'll tell Mom and Dad. But we won't tell anyone else. All right?"

"All right. Now we need to draw up a contract. It won't be legal or anything, but it'll put our plan down in writing. Then we'll both be sure of the rules we have to follow. And I think we should think up a name for our scheme."

"What kind of name?" asked Chris, looking interested.

"A *code* name. Something that no one will understand but us. You know, like in spy movies. That way no one will ever guess what we're talking about if they overhear us at school. Besides." She smiled. "It makes this thing even more exciting."

"Do you have any ideas? You're much better at that kind of thing than I am."

"Let's see." Susan thought for a minute. "I've got it! How about 'The Banana Split Affair'? After all, those are the stakes we're playing for."

"The Banana Split Affair," Chris repeated with a grin. "I love it!"

"All right. Then 'The Banana Split Affair' it is." She wrote it at the top of the page.

"One final thing," Chris said. "We both have to *promise* to carry this through. Completely. One hundred percent. No matter what happens, we won't spill the beans. Not to *anyone*, under any circumstances."

Susan hesitated. "Well, okay. I guess I'll write that into our contract, then."

"Great! Let's shake on it!" The girls shook hands, then collapsed into hysterical laughter once again.

"We'd better get started," said Susan when she finally caught her breath. "We still have a lot to do. And we only have an hour or so before dinner. Changing me into Christine Pratt isn't exactly going to be the easiest thing in the world!"

"The same goes for changing me into you, too. Hey,

Sooz, can you teach me how to paint like you in half an hour?"

"I'll have to teach you how to fake it. I have a feeling that Susan Pratt is going to develop a sudden passion for modern art in her painting class at school."

"Good. Because drawing triangles and squiggles is about all that *Christine* Pratt can handle!"

"How about math? You know that trigonometry is my worst subject. And your very best. Can you turn me into Albert Einstein by tomorrow?"

Chris rolled her eyes. "It won't be easy. But I guess I'll have to try."

"We sure have a lot to do, then! Let's get going right away."

"We'll do you first, okay? Come try on my new jeans. I think they'll fit you just fine, Sooz. I mean Chris!"

The girls started for Chris's bedroom, arm in arm. They were still caught up in the excitement of their plan.

Chris said, "You know, Sooz, there's one thing I have to say about this idea of trading lives with each other."

"What's that?" asked Susan.

Chris grinned at her sister. "This plan of ours is so outrageously crazy, my dear twin, so wildly off-the-wall and totally bizarre, that it just might work!"

Three

For the next hour the sound of laughter mixed with
muffled bits of serious conversation emerged from
behind the closed doors of one or the other of the twins'
bedrooms. The girls tried their best to be quiet, planning
to hide their little secret from their parents until just the
right moment.

Fortunately, both parents were out of the way. Mrs.
Pratt was downstairs in the family room finishing up her
mystery book while checking on dinner every few
minutes. Mr. Pratt was out in the driveway washing the
car. Even so, Susan and Chris treated the switching of
their identities like some top-level spy mission, keeping
their voices down to a whisper when they weren't
overcome with giggles. All that secrecy made it that
much more fun.

"Here are all my fall and winter clothes," Chris said,
pulling open the door of her closet. She was hardly the
neatest girl in the world, since her dates and club
meetings and long telephone conversations kept her too
busy for much serious cleaning. The top of her desk was

piled high with papers and books, and her dresser was cluttered with so many bottles and jars that it looked as if they were about to fall off. The pale blue wallpaper sprigged with tiny white flowers was covered with school banners and dance programs and math papers with big red A's at the top. Even her furry brown teddy bear had ended up on the floor in the corner.

But her closet was the one exception. Everything hung neatly side by side, blouses with blouses, skirts with skirts. Chris loved clothes and treated them like valuable possessions. She even hung up her bright tee shirts, forming a rainbow of color between her sweaters and her dresses.

"Feel free to help yourself. There's no reason why everything shouldn't fit. And you know what I usually wear." She handed Susan her new pair of jeans.

"Right. Jeans and a tee shirt or sweater shouldn't be too difficult to manage." Susan grinned.

"You'll see," Chris returned, pretending to be offended. "There's nothing more comfortable. Even though I wear my jeans a bit tight. How do those fit?"

"Ow! I can't breathe! I can barely zip these up!"

"Good," her sister said matter-of-factly. "Then they fit perfectly. That's just how I like to wear them."

"What am I getting myself into?" Susan wailed. "Do you really walk around in these things eighteen hours a day?"

"Quiet. You look great. And you'll get used to it. Now here's a tee shirt. Robin's-egg blue, one of my favorites. Don't you dare get it dirty!"

"I promise I won't even sweat in it. Since I can't breathe anyway . . ."

"We'll have to set your hair with electric rollers to make it wavy by dinnertime. Then we'll put in these blue combs."

A few minutes later Chris led her sister over to the full-length mirror that lined her bedroom door. "There!" she cried. "I've created a masterpiece!"

"Wow!" Susan exclaimed, blinking at her reflection. "Is that really *me*?"

Chris had duplicated her own hair and makeup, as well as her usual style of dress, in her sister. Standing side by side and looking into the mirror, they both felt as if they had double vision.

"Look at that!" Chris laughed. "It's you, disguised as me! It's perfect, don't you think?"

"It's *spooky*!" Susan cried. "We haven't looked this much the same since we were little, when Mom used to dress us up in the same clothes and braid our hair in pigtails the exact same way!"

"And now the finishing touch. If anybody has any doubts, this'll convince them. I guarantee it." She fastened an ID bracelet around her sister's wrist. It was a delicate gold chain, and dangling from it was a thin disc inscribed in script with the name Christine. It had been a gift from the girls' grandmother on their fifteenth birthday.

"That's a great idea, Chris. Don't let me forget to give you my heart locket with my initials on it."

She looked at the girl in the mirror once again. "I can't believe it. I just can't believe it."

"Okay. Let's do me now," Chris insisted. "If you can bear to tear yourself away from your own reflection. Christine Pratt may have many faults, but obsessive vanity is not one of them!"

The twins proceeded to Susan's bedroom, where they made another magical transformation. After a few minutes it was Chris who stared into the mirror in disbelief.

"The Banana Split Affair has begun!" she cried. With her straight hair, freshly washed face, and pale blue skirt with a flowered blouse, she had become Susan Pratt. At least on the outside.

"Here comes the hard part," said Chris, once she was able to tear herself away from her reflection. "Exchanging clothes and hairstyles is nothing. But learning each other's mannerisms and the way each of us would react in certan situations—that's going to be tricky business."

"I know," Susan agreed. "The only saving grace is that you and I have been living under the same roof for sixteen years. I do know *something* about you. And imitating you shouldn't be too hard."

She immediately launched into her best Chris Pratt act, changing her voice and her stance just enough to copy her sister. "Why should *I* kiss *you*, you silly thing? I've got hundreds of boyfriends, and every one of them is nicer and better-looking and more interesting than you!"

"I don't sound like that, Sooz!" Chris laughed. "Or do I?"

"Not the words, maybe, but I've got the voice down perfectly. Now, watch me walk like you." Susan-as-Chris strutted across the room, chin held high, arms swinging by her side.

"Oh, no!" Chris groaned, covering her eyes. "I don't walk like *that*, do I?"

"Well, not quite, I guess. But that's the idea. I'll tone it down for school. Now, what about you? Can you imitate me?"

Chris modestly folded her hands across her lap and lowered her eyes. "Mr. Douglas," she cooed in a low voice, "if I only get a ninety-nine on this history test, it'll ruin my average. You know I've never gotten less than a hundred before in my life!"

"Oh, stop!" Susan cried. "I'm not like that!"

"I know. But I had to do *something* to get back at you! Okay, I think we've got that down. You're right—after being together all our lives, there's no problem with copying each other's voice and mannerisms. What about our reactions to things?"

"What exactly do you mean? Give me an example."

"Let's see. Here's one. What would you do if a boy you'd never seen before smiled at you and started walking in your direction?"

Susan thought for a minute. "Honestly? Do you want to know what I'd really do?"

"Sure. I've got to learn more about the way you think. How can I become Susan Pratt if I don't know everything about her?"

"Well," Susan said, lowering her eyes, "I'd probably start walking in the opposite direction, as fast as I could." She glanced up at her sister. "How about you? What would you do?"

"Why, I'd smile back and wait for him, of course!"

The two girls laughed.

"I can see there are some very big differences between you and me!" Susan exclaimed.

"That's for sure."

"Uh, Chris, I guess there's something I should tell you, since we plan to go all the way with this."

"Oh, boy. This sounds juicy! What is it?"

"I, um, have kind of this . . . this *crush* on one particular guy at school." Susan blushed.

"Oh, is *that* all. Well, you'd better tell me who it is."

"Are you actually going to go after him?" Susan gasped.

"Of course," Chris said matter-of-factly. When she saw the look of horror that crossed her sister's face, she added, "In the same way that *Susan* Pratt would, of course. Although," she said with a twinkle in her brown eyes, "I just might add a bit of the old Christine charm for good measure!"

"Don't you dare!" Susan cried. "Don't forget who you are. I mean who you're *supposed* to be!"

"Trust me." Chris grinned. "I won't do anything to embarrass you. I might even end up playing match-maker." Her eyes still shone mischievously, however, and Susan wondered if telling her sister about her crush was a good idea after all. "So who is the lucky guy?"

"His name is Keith West. He's in my art class."

"What's he like? I have to be able to recognize him."

"Oooh, he's wonderful! He has sandy blond hair, and the greenest eyes you ever saw. And he's a really talented artist. Much better than I am. At least, I think so. He's nice, and smart, and kind of quiet, like me. . . ."

"Sounds like Superman."

"He's also very, very shy. Especially around girls."

Chris sighed. "I'll do what I can. I've run into the shy type before."

"Chris, please don't overdo it!"

"Don't worry. I'll still be acting like Susan Pratt." She glanced at Susan's watch, which she was wearing on her own wrist. "Hey, it's almost dinnertime. We'd better hurry. Let me give you a quick rundown of the guys I've been going out with lately."

Susan groaned. "We'll need about two hours for that!"

Chris took a playful swat at her sister. "You just wait and see, Susan Pratt! You seem to have this idea that my life is nothing but a bed of roses. Just wait until school tomorrow. *You'll* find out!"

As Chris listed all the names of the boys who had taken her out to school dances and football games and movies since school had started a few weeks earlier, Susan thought, Yes, I guess I *will* find out. That's the whole idea of this exchange, isn't it? And to be perfectly honest, *I can't wait*!

Four

"*Are you ready?*" *Chris whispered as she and Susan* made their way down the stairs toward the dining room. "This is our first big test. If we can fool Mom and Dad during dinner, we're halfway there."

"It's not quite that simple, I'm afraid," Susan said softly. "Fooling them is one thing. Getting them to okay the Banana Split Affair is something else. There's a good chance they won't be as excited about our brainstorm as we are."

"Have faith, Sooz. I've got my arguments all thought out. Don't forget, I used to be on the Debating Team. If I can't convince them that our plan is terrific, no one can."

"Great," her sister groaned. "If you can't convince them that our plain is terrific, then I show up at school tomorrow morning as good old Susan Pratt. Just as always. And we're right back where we started."

"*Trust* me!" In a normal tone of voice, Chris, wearing her Susan Pratt identity, said, "Hi, Mom. Hi, Dad. Is dinner about ready?"

"Sit right down," said her mother. "Or better yet, come on into the kitchen and help serve. You too, Chris."

The girls grinned at each other. While their mother hadn't taken the time to look at them very carefully, she had nevertheless been fooled by the girls' clothing, makeup, and hairstyles. She just assumed that the wavy-haired twin in the bright tee shirt was Chris and that the other twin, hair straight and clothing subdued, was Susan. Both of them were encouraged by their first minor success. Chris-as-Susan held up both hands with her fingers crossed.

As they sat down to dinner and chatted with their parents, both girls were tense. Talking and acting like each other was a task that called for constant attention. Still, no one seemed to notice that anything was out of the ordinary.

Every once in a while, Chris and Susan glanced at each other nervously.

"How do you think we're doing?" Susan-as-Chris's eyes asked her twin.

"Relax," was the response that Chris-as-Susan's calm expression said. "We're doing fine. Neither Dad nor Mom suspects anything."

The meal went smoothly as the family listened to Mr. Pratt's account of the trouble he'd had with the car lately and Mrs. Pratt filled them in on the latest happenings at the gourmet housewares shop she managed. But then the conversation became more personal, and the difficulties began.

"Chris, dear, did you change your clothes?" Mrs. Pratt suddenly noticed her daughter's outfit. She looked confused as she eyed her blue tee shirt and jeans.

The real Chris poked Susan in the ribs. "Mom asked you a question, Chris."

"O-oh. I'm sorry. I guess I was daydreaming. What'd you say, Mom?"

"Am I going crazy, or were you wearing that bright yellow tee shirt before? With those brown corduroy pants of yours?"

This time Susan was alert. "Yes, I did change. I, um, spilled baby powder all over my clothes."

"Baby powder! What on earth were you doing with baby powder?"

Susan was about to stutter out an answer when Chris interrupted. "She didn't have time to wash her hair before dinner, so she brushed baby powder through it. You know, like a dry shampoo."

"Oh." Mrs. Pratt continued to look puzzled. "But aren't you going to wash your hair later?"

Susan blurted out her response. "Yes, but in the meantime, it felt dirty. And, well, you know how I feel about eating dinner with dirty hair."

Mrs. Pratt glanced at her quizzically. "I've never heard of that one, Chris. This must be a new obsession of yours. Like when you were thirteen and would wear only the color white because you'd read in some magazine that girls with dark hair looked best in pale colors."

"That's Chris for you," the real Chris mumbled, pretending to be absorbed in picking up stray pieces of rice from her plate with her fork.

Mrs. Pratt then looked at her other daughter. A frown crossed her face. "Come to think of it, Susan, weren't you wearing something else before, too?"

"Well, yeah, but I spilled paint on my other clothes."

"My goodness! What is this, a contest to see which twin can create the most laundry?"

"Oh, you know what klutzes sixteen-year-old girls can be," Chris said offhandedly. "Always dropping things, spilling stuff all over the place . . . Must be growing pains." She couldn't resist catching Susan's eye and grinning.

Their mother shook her head. "I've never heard of anything like that before. Especially with you two. Must be some new phase you're going through. Chris, would you please pass the gravy?"

Susan continued eating, ignoring her mother's request.

"Chris, hon, the gravy?"

No response.

"Christine," Mr. Pratt said, "would you please come down from Cloud Nine long enough to pass the gravy to your mother? Or is living on another planet also part of these mysterious 'growing pains' that seem to have overtaken my daughters all of a sudden?"

Susan finally looked up. "What?"

"Oh, here, I'll pass the gravy." Chris came to the rescue. She kicked her twin under the table. "*Christine*," she said, "would you please pay attention? People are going to start wondering what's wrong with you."

"Sorry. I guess I was thinking about my painting."

"What painting?" both parents chorused.

Another kick under the table. "What Chris means," the real Chris said through clenched teeth, "is that she's decided to try her hand at watercolors. I'm going to teach her." She glared at her sister. Susan looked back apologetically.

"I think that's a tremendous idea." Their father smiled as he helped himself to more string beans. "Susan is such an accomplished artist that it'd be great if she'd share some of that ability with Chris."

Chris smiled. "I have a feeling Chris'll be a fast learner. I don't know why; it's just a gut reaction."

"Giving art lessons is fine," Mrs. Pratt said, "just as long as everyone gets her homework done first. That reminds me—don't you have a history test tomorrow, Chris? I don't mean to nag, but you know history isn't exactly your best subject."

"I'm ready for this exam, though," Susan-as-Chris assured her. "I bet I'll even get an A."

Her father looked doubtful. "That'd be fine, Chris, but don't set your goals too high. The pressure will make it that much tougher. Besides, haven't you been doing B and C work in history all along? I don't want you to be too disappointed."

"I've got a C average right now." Susan-as-Chris grinned. "But trust me. I know this stuff cold. I can practically guarantee that I'll get an A."

"It's good to think positively, Chris," Mrs. Pratt said gently, "but . . ."

"I've been coached by Susan," Susan explained. "And you know that history is one of her best subjects."

"I'm glad you're so confident. And we certainly wish you the best of luck on your test." Mrs. Pratt stood up from the table. "Now, how about some dessert? There's still half of that apple pie left over from last night. I've got it warming in the oven. And as a special treat, your father picked up some vanilla ice cream to put on top."

"Not me," Chris said automatically. "You know about my obsession with getting fat. Especially with my new jea . . ."

"Honestly, Susan," Susan interrupted her in a voice that was much too loud, "you're beginning to sound just like me. All this talk about getting fat." This time it was Susan's turn to kick her twin under the table.

Mr. Pratt leaned back in his chair and crossed his arms. "Is it my imagination, or is something strange going on here? Susan? Chris? Are you both acting peculiar, or is all this just some part of teenage girls growing up that I never read about in psychology books?"

"Whatever do you mean, Daddy?" Chris asked innocently, her brown eyes open wide.

"I'm not sure." He narrowed his eyes and peered at each one of the twins. "It's nothing concrete, just sort of a . . . a *hunch* I have. I've been getting mixed signals from you both ever since we sat down to dinner."

"Yes," Mrs. Pratt agreed. "I've noticed, too. Are you two up to something? Chris, you're the usual prankster. Are you planning something . . . Oh, my goodness!"

Mrs. Pratt threw back her head and laughed.

"For heaven's sake! You two! . . . If I hadn't seen it for myself, I never would have believed it!"

"Not you, too!" her husband groaned. "What on earth is going on here? Or is it so obvious that everyone can see it but me?" He glanced from Susan to Chris to his wife. All three of them were laughing.

"My dear Mr. Pratt, kindly take a close look at your daughters. One at a time."

"I thought we'd already been through that. Both of them change their clothes as often as Barbie Dolls, and Christine wears white powder in her hair as if she were doing an imitation of George Washington."

"Look *closely*," Mrs. Pratt insisted.

"I still don't understand . . . Oh, my gosh!"

Mrs. Pratt stood behind him and threw her arms around his neck. "Remember how we used to tell them apart? Chris had that tiny beauty mark on her left cheek."

"I see what you mean!" Mr. Pratt chuckled. "What is *Susan* doing with *Christine*'s beauty mark on her face? *Now* I understand. Goodness, you two are impossible!"

"I don't know about you, but I feel kind of foolish. Imagine not being able to tell my own two daughters apart!"

"Well, we *are* identical twins," Chris reminded her. "Besides, we made a special effort to disguise ourselves as each other. But we forgot all about the beauty mark." She turned to Susan. "Sooz, we'll have to remember to take care of that with a little makeup."

"Take care of that for what?" Mr. Pratt asked. "Are you two mischief makers thinking of trying this charade again? Maybe playing a practical joke on a boyfriend or on one of your teachers at school?"

Chris and Susan exchanged glances. Suddenly they had doubts about their plan. Or at least about telling their parents about it.

But Susan took a deep breath and said, "Chris and I have developed a kind of . . . *experiment*."

"Experiment?" her mother repeated.

"It's called the Banana Split Affair," Chris interjected. "Like in spy movies. Doesn't it sound mysterious?"

"*Very* mysterious. And slightly dangerous. You two aren't planning anything illegal, are you?" Mr. Pratt joked, pretending to be horrified. "I'd hate to have the FBI after us. All those unmarked cars and trench coats— why, the very thought gives me the heebie-jeebies!"

"We're not doing anything illegal," Susan assured him. "Merely educational."

"Well, I'm certainly in favor of anything that's educational," her father said. "But I would like some more details, if you don't mind."

"It's simple," Chris explained. "Sooz and I are

identical twins, but we're both completely different people. And since we have the same face and the same birthday and everything else that twins share, it's only natural that we would wonder what it'd be like to be the other." With a dramatic wave of her hand, she announced, "So we came up with the obvious solution! Enter, the Banana Split Affair!"

"We've decided to change places for a while," Susan went on. "I am now Christine Pratt, and my twin here is Susan Pratt. So you see, it *is* educational."

Mrs. Pratt looked doubtful. "Are you sure this is a good idea, girls? I know I'm always telling you both that you're old enough to make your own decisions and that learning to run your own lives is important, but . . ."

"And just how long is 'a while'?" the girls' father wanted to know.

"It's only for two weeks," Susan said hesitantly. She was beginning to see that her parents weren't quite as enthusiastic about the Banana Split Affair as she and Chris were. "Not very long at all."

"We hoped you'd think it was as inspired an idea as we did," Chris added. "After all, you're always telling us how important it is to learn about human nature and understand other people and live by the Golden Rule and all that."

"This hardly sounds like a way of learning about the Golden Rule." Mr. Pratt sighed. "I don't know about this. What do *you* think?" he asked his wife.

Mrs. Pratt thought for a minute. "Well, I can't say I approve one hundred percent. It *is* kind of a clever idea, though, and we've got to give the girls credit for thinking it up and carrying it off so well that it fooled even us.

"On the one hand, I suppose they could get into

trouble by switching identities. Especially at school. They'd be taking tests for each other. . . ."

"But one test wouldn't make much difference in our final averages," Chris protested.

"Besides," Susan added, "we could always tell our teachers what we did after the two weeks were up."

"True. Then there's the other side," their mother went on. "Chris and Susan managed to fool us, so there's no reason why they couldn't go ahead and trade identities without our knowing. Once they get to school, we have no inkling of what's going on."

"We'd never do it if you forbade us," Susan said quickly.

Chris gave her a dirty look.

"I know that," Mrs. Pratt said with a smile. "I know I can count on you girls. But if you want my honest opinion"—she shrugged—"I don't see anything wrong with it. Not as long as the girls don't get carried away. And I do trust them. They're smart enough and mature enough to be able to handle something like this. I also agree with Susan that it would be educational for them. Not to mention an awful lot of fun."

The girls grinned at each other, eyes shining.

"What about you, Daddy?" Chris asked. "Do you agree with Mom?"

He looked around the table at the three pairs of eyes that were watching him intently, waiting for his answer. He shook his head slowly and said, "Who am I to go against the wishes of the three females in my life? You all know what a pushover I am for a beautiful woman." He winked at his wife. "I never was very good at saying no."

"Oh, Daddy!" the twins squealed, rushing over to

him and smothering him with hugs and kisses. "Thank you! Thank you!"

Susan turned to her mother and gave her a hug. "We'll be careful, Mom. We won't do anything that'll get us into trouble."

"I know," Mrs. Pratt said, returning the squeeze. "As I said before, I trust you both. You're sensible, level-headed girls. . . ."

Just then Chris knocked over a half-filled glass of water as she threw her arms around her father's neck. She jumped back with a gasp.

After a second of total silence, all four Pratts burst out laughing.

"That's my girls." Mr. Pratt chuckled, setting the glass right. "'Sensible, levelheaded . . .'"

"We'll do fine!" the twins assured him. "You'll see!"

Chris and Susan clasped hands in a firm handshake. "Well, we did it! We got Mom and Dad to approve our scheme!" Chris exclaimed gleefully.

"Right!" cried Susan. "The Banana Split Affair is on!"

Five

The next morning Susan and Chris were so excited about going to school and trying out their new identities that they couldn't even eat breakfast.

"Please! At least have a glass of milk!" their mother pleaded, following them around with a half-gallon carton. "Or let me make you some toast to eat while you're walking to school!"

"There isn't time," Chris insisted. "It took us so long to get Sooz's hair just right that we'll be late if we don't leave right now. We've got to hurry."

"This is the first time I've ever seen you so concerned about getting to school on time. How about you, Susan?"

"I'm Chris, remember?" teased Susan. "And I have to get going, too."

"How about some toast, Chris?—wait a minute—I mean *Susan*. I'll be darned if I'm going to start calling my own two daughters by the wrong names!"

"You'll get used to it." Chris gave her a peck on the

cheek. "Come on, Chris," she called to Susan. "Got everything? Your trigonometry book? Your history notes?"

"Oh, my," Mrs. Pratt clucked, shaking her head. "I don't think I had any idea what I was saying last night when I agreed to this idea. I don't know how I'll ever manage to get through these two weeks!"

"Then think how *we* must feel!" The real Susan grinned. "Talk about confusing! *I* don't even know who I really am!" She turned to her sister. "I'm ready, Sooz. Here I come." She trotted after her, through the kitchen and out the back door.

"Now, remember," the real Chris began as the two of them started the short walk to school. "Don't do *too* well on that history test. We don't want to be too obvious. And don't forget that instead of regular gym third period, the class is going to the auditorium to see a hygiene film."

"I've got it down pat," Susan assured her. "Just so I won't forget, I've got your whole schedule written down. I took some notes last night."

"That figures! Good old organized Susan!" her twin teased.

"Hey, wait a minute! Let me say something in my own defense. Just listen to this list of names I'm supposed to keep straight." She read from a piece of loose-leaf paper covered with her neat handwriting. "*Greg*—two dates. *Michael*—Welcome Dance. Possibly Homecoming Dance. *Alan*—flirts a lot in trig but hasn't called yet. *Bruce* . . ."

"All right, all right. I take it back. Now, as far as me pretending to be you, the main thing I have to remember is to sweep this Keith West off his feet, right?"

Susan remained silent, but her jaw was clenched. She

had pleaded with Chris all night to make sure she didn't overdo it, and she had no desire to start up again. It was out of her hands.

Besides, she told herself, maybe Chris would be able to do some good where she had failed. As far as she knew, Keith West thought of her as just one more nameless face who sat somewhere behind him in art class and wandered over now and then to make some dumb comment about how much she liked his projects. So maybe Chris's self-confidence and ease with boys would end up doing her some good in the long run.

As they reached the school yard, the girls exchanged nervous glances.

"Well," Chris breathed, "this is it. Do I look all right?"

"You look perfect," Susan assured her. "You look just like me."

"And you look just like me. I feel like I'm looking into a mirror. Well . . . good luck, *Chris*."

"Good luck to you, *Sooz*."

"See you at lunch!"

Susan dashed off to her homeroom. She was relieved that the last bell rang just as she arrived, leaving her only enough time to slide into her seat. She pretended to be absorbed in her history notes so that no one would talk to her. Homeroom was the one area that Chris had forgotten to fill her in on.

She nervously read through her copy of Chris's schedule for the hundredth time. Fifth period was English. That should be easy enough, since it was one of Susan's best subjects. Gym was next. No problem there. Then came trigonometry, the class she was most worried about. At fourth-period lunch, she would meet Chris and compare notes on how the morning had gone.

"Oh, well," she sighed as the bell rang and she joined the crowd of students who shuffled out of the classroom, "better to get it over with than sit around worrying. Here goes." Her heart was beating wildly, since she was somewhere between excited and scared.

It wasn't until she walked out into the hall on her way to first-period English that Susan got her first taste of what being Christine Pratt was like. So many students waved or called "hello" that she felt like a celebrity. The faces of Chris's friends and acquaintances passed by in a blur, most of them belonging to students she didn't know and had never even noticed before. But many were those of the school's leaders: Sally Linder, class president. Ralph Maxwell, head of the debating team. Fred Davis, captain of the football team. The kind of people who were only vaguely aware that Susan Pratt existed. And that was only because she happened to be the twin sister of the popular Christine Pratt.

The new Chris simply smiled and waved back. She wasn't certain of most people's names, and she wasn't about to risk ruining things by making mistakes. But one thing was for sure: She *loved* getting so much attention, and from so many important kids, too! It was a far cry from being her usual self, staying close to the lockers that lined the crowded halls and avoiding eye contact with anyone but her closest friends. She found herself standing up straighter and wearing a constant smile. This was fun!

As she turned down a corridor, she heard someone calling her.

"Chris! Chris! Hey, wait up!"

Susan turned around and saw Richard Collier running after her. Her smile immediately started to fade. Richard was one boy she knew only too well. He was one of

Chris's regulars, and Susan had never been able to understand what her sister saw in him. But she put on her biggest smile and braced herself. Like it or not, she would have to flirt with Richard. After all, the real Chris certainly would.

"Hiya, Chris! What's the rush? Or are you trying to compete with your sister for the Goody Two Shoes Award by being on time for class?"

Susan's mouth dropped open. She could feel her cheeks burning. She had never particularly *liked* Richard, but she had never known him to be cruel. Was this what Richard Collier was *really* like? Then what on earth did Chris *see* in him? Especially when she had her choice of practically every boy at school?

But she knew she couldn't let on, as hurt and disgusted as she was. Instead, Susan forced herself to continue smiling. "Don't be such a meanie," she said in her best Chris voice. She stroked her hair in the nervous habit that her twin always used. "Just because my sister happens to be a better student than either you or me . . ."

"Aw, forget it. I don't want to talk about your sister. I want to talk about Friday night."

"What about Friday night?"

"Don't tell me my best girl has forgotten about the party at Slade's already?" He draped his arm around her casually. It was all Susan could do to keep from pulling away.

"Actually," she said in the most teasing voice she could manage, "I have such a busy social calendar that I can't remember *what's* on for Friday night. Maybe you'd better refresh my memory."

"Goodness, girl, are you losing your mind? I told you you've been studying too much lately."

As she eyed the tall, wiry boy with slick black hair and a gaunt face, Susan wondered once again what Chris saw in him. She also knew she had no desire to go to a party or anywhere else with him. Especially at the house of someone named Slade whom she had never heard of.

"Funny you should say that," she said, purposely dropping a textbook on the floor and escaping from his grasp to pick it up. "My mom's really been cracking down lately about me going out so much. She wants me to put in more time studying."

"Even on the weekends? Come on, babe. You'll destroy me!"

"Why don't you call me, Richard? I've got to run or I'll be late for my first-period class. We're having a test," she lied.

"Okay. I'll call you tonight. Right after dinner. But you'd better say yes to Slade's blast! The whole gang's counting on you!"

Susan was relieved when she reached the safety of the English classroom. Ms. Long was generally a kind teacher, but she was known for lighting into students who weren't lucky enough to be her favorites. Susan had already studied *An American Tragedy* in her English class the previous year, so she felt confident that she would be well prepared for any class discussion or even a surprise quiz.

She checked her notes to see which seat was Chris's. As she sat down, the girl next to her gave her a big smile and a friendly "hello." Susan surmised she was a friend of Chris's, but she had no idea who she was. It was just as well that her unexpected—and unwanted—encounter with Richard Collier had left her no time to chat with any of the other students before class got started.

Just as Chris had told her, the class was discussing the

theme of *An American Tragedy*. The book was one of Susan's favorites, and she sat up straight and listened intently to the discussion. When Ms. Long asked about the meaning of the novel, Susan's hand automatically shot up.

"Now, there's a hand I don't have the pleasure of seeing too often," Ms. Long remarked. "I guess someone has finally caught up with the assignment! Christine, what words of wisdom have *you* got to share with us about the meaning of the book?"

Susan blanched, then took a deep breath. She could feel everyone's eyes upon her, and she immediately realized that the class was just as surprised as Ms. Long that the usually quiet and uninterested Chris Pratt was about to answer a question.

"Dreiser felt it was a myth that anyone could rise in American society. When poor Clyde tried to make a better life for himself, he ended up being tricked by circumstance. He was a victim. You could even say that the price he had to pay for trying to step out of his social class was his life."

"That's very good, Chris. I'm glad you got so much out of the book. It seems to mean a great deal to you. I must say I'm as pleased as I am surprised." Ms. Long's eyes traveled around the classroom. "Does anyone have anything to add to Christine's comment?"

Susan was taken aback by Ms. Long's reaction. Susan-as-Susan was always raising her hand and giving good answers to questions in almost all her classes. But the English teacher had acted as if she were amazed that Susan-as-Chris had anything at all to say. That she was even capable of understanding the books the class was reading.

It must be harder for Chris than I realized, she thought

as the class discussion continued around her. I guess a lot of times she doesn't know the answers to things that are being talked about in class. I wonder if she feels bad about that. And I wonder if she's always worried about getting called on and maybe embarrassing herself in front of everybody.

Before she had too much time to think about her sister's feeling as a C student, a new difficulty came up. The girl sitting next to her, the one who had acted so friendly when she came into the classroom, slipped her a folded piece of loose-leaf paper while Ms. Long was writing on the blackboard.

"Dear Chris," the note read. "Three guesses who FINALLY asked Carla out!!!"

Susan swallowed hard. She had no idea who *Carla* was, let alone the name of any boys who might have asked her out. What could she do? Make up names? Ask for an explanation? Neither would do. Her twin sister was obviously very familiar with all the details of this Carla's social life.

She thought for a few seconds. And then, *inspiration!* Making sure she imitated Chris's handwriting as best she could, she scribbled at the bottom of the note, "You're kidding! FINALLY!!!" and handed it back to her neighbor. The girl glanced at it, then looked over at Susan. She rolled her eyes and grinned knowingly. Susan copied her reaction, trying to look as amazed as she possibly could.

During the rest of the period, Susan waited in dread for the girl to pass her another note. Fortunately, Ms. Long started to wander around the classroom as she lead the discussion, so there was no chance for writing any more secret messages. Susan decided not to answer any more questions, as tempting as it was. *She* knew the answer, but would *Chris*? Better not to take a chance. She was beginning to realize that while she, Susan, tried not to be noticed in social situations, Chris did the exact same thing in school. How odd that she had never thought of that before!

If the Banana Split Affair is supposed to teach me about Chris's life, she thought at the end of the period as she gathered up her books and hurried out of the classroom with a quick wave in the strange girl's direction, it's already starting to do the job!

Her next class was gym. That was easy. Following Chris's instructions, she went to the auditorium and sat in the dark, watching a hygiene film. She sat at the end of the row, and the girl sitting next to her didn't appear to be a friend of Chris's. Susan felt she could breathe freely for the first time that day.

Trigonometry was a bit more difficult. Every time the math teacher, Mr. James, asked a question, especially one that was especially hard, Susan-as-Chris could feel his eyes upon her. She looked everywhere but at him— out the window, in her purse, in the textbook. She got away without being called on once. It was a good thing, too, since all that talk about tangents and cosines made her head throb. It was as if she were hearing a different language. At the end of the period, she rushed out, hoping Mr. James would just assume she was having a bad day. She would have to talk to Chris about this one! Two weeks of looking as if she weren't paying attention would be no easy feat! And it wouldn't exactly help Chris in the long run, either!

Susan was relieved that it was finally time for lunch period. But her relief didn't last long.

As she strolled into the school cafeteria, she spotted her twin sitting at a table full of Susan Pratt's friends.

That left her only one alternative: to respond to Sally Linder, the junior class president, who was waving at her, trying to catch her attention.

"Chris! Hey, Chris! Over here!"

Susan's stomach sank. She hesitated for a moment, then walked over to Sally's table.

"Hi, Chris, I see you're brown-bagging it today. Me, too. I'm on a diet." Sally grimaced for effect. "How was your date with Tommy Turner yesterday?"

Susan-as-Chris sat down and unwrapped her sandwich. "Uh, it was great. Really fun." She glanced around the table at the four other girls, who were watching her intently. Two or three of them looked vaguely familiar, but she had no idea of their names. She could feel herself growing warm. This was going to be tough. Maybe even the toughest thing she had to do so far.

"Hey, Chris," one of the other girls said, peering at her across the table, "you look different today. I can't quite put my finger on why, but there's something about you . . ."

"Oh," said Susan with a wave of her hand, hoping her cheeks weren't turning *too* red, "it's probably my hair. I tried something different with it. And I'm wearing my sister's makeup."

"Really? I didn't even know your sister even wore any makeup," Sally said offhandedly, turning to her plastic container of cottage cheese.

"Actually, Susan is prettier than I am," she mumbled in her own defense. "She doesn't need much makeup."

"How can that be?" asked another of the nameless girls. "I thought you two were identical twins."

"We are, but there are differences in coloring, the shape of our faces . . ."

"Well, nothin' against your sister, Chris, but I think you're much prettier. Not to mention the fact that you dress a lot better."

"But what's more important is that you're so much more bubbly," another girl added. "Your sister is probably just as nice as you, and I've heard she's really smart and all, but she just doesn't come across the way you do . . . you know, confident and friendly and interesting. The kind of person everyone wants to get to know. You can tell that Chris Pratt *likes* herself."

Instead of feeling offended, Susan was taking mental notes. So *that* was what made Chris so popular! It had nothing to do with her looks after all. The secret was that Chris really liked herself. And that made people like her. Everyone thought Chris was nicer and more interesting than her twin sister—it was as simple as that. It made sense, of course, but somehow Susan had never thought of it in those terms.

The conversation drifted away from the Pratt twins and onto school politics, the new hamburger joint that had just opened near school, and speculation over who the new replacement cheerleader would be. Between eating and offering little or few comments, Susan was able to continue convincing everyone at the table that she was Chris. Still, when Sally glanced at the clock and noted that the period was almost over, Susan breathed a sigh of relief.

She made sure she ran into her sister on the way out of the cafeteria.

"Well," she said to Chris as the two of them filed out together, "I managed to make it through the day so far. But I think lunch was the hardest. How about you? Did you get through lunch okay?"

"Just barely! I just kept my mouth shut as much as

possible. You know, I feel kind of bad fooling our friends like that. Don't you?"

Susan just grinned. "No, not at all! I think it's terrific that we managed to trick them! After all, they know us the best, so they're the hardest group to convince. If we fooled them, we can fool anybody!"

"I guess you're right," Chris finally agreed. "I feel like an actress who just made a theaterful of people believe she was Juliet. It was bad enough in class, but your friends were sitting six inches away from me!"

"Speaking of Juliet," Susan said, biting her lip, "there's still one more category of people we have to convince before we can say that we've been one hundred percent successful."

"Who's that?"

"The Romeos in our lives."

"Oh, yeah, boys. I forgot about them. And I have your art class next period, right?"

Susan nodded. She was so concerned about the present that she forgot to mention her odd meeting with Richard Collier. "Right," she said, "art is next. And your mission is to make Keith West fall madly in love with Susan Pratt. Even if she really is Christine Pratt."

"Well," Chris said a bit nervously, "I'll give it my best shot. That's all I can do. Wish me luck!"

"Good luck!" Susan exclaimed, patting her sister on the back.

I really mean it, too, she thought as she watched her sister walk away toward the art studio. I'm already waiting for fifth period to be over so I can find out what happened! One thing is certain: I hope that Chris-as-Susan has better luck in catching Keith West's eye than Susan-as-Susan has!

Six

*Chris sat at a desk covered with a pad of thick-*textured paper, a plastic cup filled with water, a handful of fine brushes, and three tubes of watercolor paint. She eyed the art materials warily.

How on earth am I going to get through the next forty minutes of Susan's art class? she wondered. Not only do I have to figure out exactly what to do with those strange things that are as foreign to me as Indian fossils. I also have to convince Mr. Smith, the art teacher, and the fifteen students in this class that I'm the talented, well-trained Susan Pratt.

"Today I'd like you to try something different," Mr. Smith was saying. "Something that will stretch your creativity a little bit more than the more standard kinds of projects you've been working on so far this semester."

A murmur of excitement swept through the room. Chris's frown only deepened.

Terrific, she thought morosely. I'm about as creative as a marble statue. Here I'd hoped I could get by with a mishmash of colors that I could pass off as expression-ism. But no, today has to be the day that Susan's art instructor decides to get fancy.

"As you all know, you can walk into any art supply store in the country today and buy any tube of water paints you want. Companies like Windsor and Newton have done us the service of manufacturing every shade in the rainbow. And not only green, purple, and blue, either. Take blue, for example. You could buy yourself a tube of cerulean blue, cobalt blue, turquoise blue, bimini blue, peacock blue. . . . The list is practically end-less. Being able to choose from so many different kinds of blues makes the artist's job that much more simple.

"But what would you do if you had to mix your own colors? If all of a sudden the art-supply companies disappeared from the face of the earth and you had to go back to primitive times when people were forced to develop new shades by mixing what was available?"

"I know what *I'd* do," a male voice called out from the back of the room. "I'd switch my major to chemistry!"

The class, including Chris, laughed.

"Sorry, Phil, you won't get off so easily." Mr. Smith smiled. "Not today, anyway.

"Now, you'll all notice that besides the usual supplies for watercolor painting, I've placed three tubes of paints on each desk. As you can see, they are the three primary colors: red, blue, and yellow. Who'd like to tell me what's so special about the primary colors?"

"All colors are made up of mixtures of them," a girl volunteered.

"At least in theory!" added Phil.

"Not only in theory, Phil. It also happens to be true in reality. What I want you to do today is make a painting using as many colors as you would under ordinary circumstances. But the trick is to mix them all from the three tubes of paint you've been given."

"Mr. Smith, will you be available after school today for extra help?" quipped a boy in the front of the room. Once again everyone laughed.

Chris felt a little bit relieved. *At least the rest of the class is as nervous as I am about this assignment,* she thought. *Maybe no one else knows how to approach this either. Too bad Susan—the* real *Susan—isn't here today. This sounds like just the kind of project she'd love. She's always coming up with these impossible ideas on her own, just to challenge herself.* She sighed. *As for me, I prefer to take the easy way out of things.*

As she gingerly picked up a paintbrush, Chris was glad to see that once Mr. Smith's short lecture ended, students felt free to wander around the classroom to discuss the project and look at one another's work. There was a comfortable atmosphere in the room that was unlike anything she had ever experienced in any other class.

No wonder Susan is so enthusiastic about her art courses, Chris thought. *I can see that something like this could really get to be fun. That is, if you have some kind of knack for it. Which I certainly don't.*

She continued to stare at the blank sheet of white paper. There was nothing really difficult in Mr. Smith's assignment, she knew. It was meant to be an experiment, a learning assignment. But somehow she couldn't manage to get started. She realized she was afraid.

Afraid! Christine Pratt? The girl who had given speeches to an entire auditoriumful of attentive students when she ran for student council office? Who had tried out for every club from cheerleading to debating to drama? Who had dated nearly every team captain, boys that most girls were too shy even to smile at? Yet as much as she tried to convince herself that there was nothing frightening about mixing a bunch of paints, she couldn't bring herself to get started.

"What's the matter, Susan?" Mr. Smith had been strolling around the classroom, glancing over people's shoulders and offering suggestions. "I'm surprised that you haven't gotten started yet. This is the kind of thing I would have expected you to throw your whole self into. Are you having trouble getting inspired?"

"I guess so, Mr. Smith. I seem to do better with the more structured kind of projects."

"Nonsense! This is really no more difficult than anything else we've done this semester. I suspect that you're just a bit shaky about confronting something as freewheeling and loose as this. But an artist can't always rely on the conventional methods. Sometimes you have to search to find the medium that best expresses what it is you want to communicate. To be able to find that medium, you must be able to step beyond the ordinary limits. That's what separates the true artist from someone who just plods along doing things that have already been done. Try loosening up!"

Loosening up! Chris started at Mr. Smith's words. Why, that was what she was always telling Susan! "Be more daring. Don't be so conventional! The safest way of approaching things is not always the best way!"

And here she was, the daring free spirit, held back by the same kind of fear. The fear of letting go, of experimenting, of possibly failing. So there was a little bit of that human weakness in her, too! It was painful to acknowledge but a lesson worth learning. From now on, besides recognizing it in herself, she would stop accusing Susan of being so timid. The only difference between them was that their fears were brought on by unrelated situations.

"Why don't you take a walk around the classroom, Susan?" Mr. Smith suggested in a friendly tone. "You might be able to conquer your 'artist's block' by looking at what some of the other students are doing."

"That's a good idea," she sighed. Then she brightened. Not only would she get to see how other people were managing to mix their paints; she would also have the opportunity to talk to Keith West, her sister's secret crush.

She stopped beside several desks, peering at people's palettes and asking questions about their techniques before pausing before what she had ascertained must be Keith's desk. Blond hair, green eyes, an expression of total absorption in his work.

"Hi, Keith," she ventured, hoping that her sister's description was accurate enough for her to pick him out of the whole class.

The boy looked up from his painting and blinked hard, as if his thoughts had been so far away that he needed a few seconds to get used to the fact that he was back on Planet Earth once again.

"Oh, hi, Susan. How's it going?"

Chris couldn't help noticing that he turned a bright shade of pink when he saw her. Was he just shy around girls, or was Susan Pratt someone special to him? She was also surprised to see that he was rather good-looking. She had assumed that her twin wasn't a very good judge of that kind of thing, but Susan, she discovered, had a good eye after all. There was something pleasing about his even features and cautious smile. The round tortoiseshell glasses he wore also suited him well. They added an air of dignity to a boy who was smart and serious but also had many more dimensions to his personality that lurked just below the surface.

"Things aren't going too well, I'm afraid. I haven't gotten started yet."

"You? Why not?"

She shrugged. "This isn't the kind of thing I'm used to doing. Mr. Smith says I have an 'artist's block' I have to get over. What he means is that I'm chicken to try something I've never done before."

"How could you possibly be afraid of anything?" Keith looked at her with genuine astonishment, his paintbrush poised in the air. "Why, you're the very best artist in the school! If not the entire state!"

"I'm so pleased to hear that you think so!" Chris was happy for her sister. At least, that was her immediate reaction. Then she realized that she was blushing over Keith's compliment and it was *Chris* who was flattered, not *Susan*. Ridiculous! she immediately scolded herself. You're Susan, remember? Keith has never even met the real Chris Pratt. Don't go getting all confused now just because a boy with sincere green eyes and a gentle way of speaking has said something nice to you!

She forced herself to stay aware of the role she was playing.

"Oh, I'm not so good," she said modestly, lowering her eyes. "I just work at my art projects really hard."

"Come on, Susan, you don't have to admit it. We both know how talented you are. What about all those awards you've won?"

"There haven't been *that* many. . . ."

"What about the principal choosing *your* painting out of the entire school's entries to put up in his office?"

"I don't know. Maybe I was just lucky."

Chris remembered when Susan had been awarded that honor, of course. But she hadn't been aware of just how important it was. Or of how proud her sister must have felt. *I guess having a lot of friends—especially a lot of boyfriends—is even less important than I thought,* she mused. *Having a talent and being rewarded for it is pretty impressive. I just never thought about how special my sister really is.*

"Anyway," she said, anxious to get away from the embarrassing subject of herself, "I happen to think you're quite an artist, too. You're terrific. Much better than I am. And whether it's recognized or not, I think *you're* the best."

This time Keith turned beet red. "Well, gee, I, uh, guess it doesn't really matter. I mean, a true artist doesn't paint for other people. He—or she—paints for himself. To soothe something burning inside so fiercely that it has to be communicated to the rest of the world."

"That's nice," Chris said dreamily. "I never really thought about it that way."

There was a short silence. As Chris was wondering whether the conversation was over, whether she should go back to her desk and leave Keith to his work, he placed his brush in the glass of water on the corner of his desk.

"Who's your favorite artist?" he asked. He spoke the words so quickly that it was obvious to Chris that he was trying to prolong their time together.

Unfortunately, Chris suddenly drew a complete blank. She didn't know very much about art as it was. And now that the pressure was on to play the role of her knowledgeable sister and impress Keith, she totally forgot what little she did know.

"Uh, it's hard to say. There are so many I like. . . ."

"Yeah, me too. But I especially like the impressionists."

"Funny you should say that," Chris said quickly. "I like them, too."

"I love their use of color."

"I do, too." Chris started to get fidgety as Keith's comments got deeper. She hoped she would be able to hold her own in this discussion. She knew that Susan would have had no trouble at all.

"Which impressionist painter do you like best?"

"Oh, I, uh, I always liked, uh . . ."

"I like Renoir," Keith interrupted. He didn't seem to notice the difficulty she was having with his simple questions.

"I *adore* Renoir!" she cried. "That's my very favorite painter!" Chris was glad she was fast-thinking enough to use the word "that," since she had no idea of whether this artist named Renoir was male or female.

"He's really terrific." Keith nodded. "I could look at his paintings forever."

"He's the greatest," Chris agreed, relieved that she had at least discovered that Renoir was a man.

After another brief hesitation, Chris said, "Well, I guess I should get back to my desk. The period's almost half-over, and I haven't even started yet."

"You know, I'm glad we had this chance to talk," Keith said, smiling shyly. "I've seen you in this art class every day for the last two months, but you've always seemed so absorbed in what you were doing that I never had the nerve to speak to you before. But now I see that not only are you a wonderful artist; you also know a lot about art!"

Again Chris was pleased at his compliment. The fact

that she had barely gotten by in her conversation with Keith about painters didn't matter. "Well, good-bye, I guess." She was surprised to discover that she was reluctant to pull herself away.

She went back to her desk, ready to tackle her paints. But as she became absorbed in squeezing blobs out onto a palette, she felt something nagging at her. A peculiar sense of confusion.

It was obvious to her that contrary to her twin's belief, Keith had been noticing her for some time. And not in any casual way, either. Keith West, as shy and quiet as he was, definitely had his eye on Susan Pratt.

It had been her mission to discover that and to encourage any interest he might have in Susan. But now that that had been accomplished, there was something else bothering her. What was it? she wondered, trying to ignore her feelings and concentrate on art class. There's something odd going on here, and I won't be able to think straight until I figure it out.

All of a sudden Chris dropped her brush. It fell across her blank sheet of paper, leaving a bright red streak across the white surface.

Oh, no! she thought, suddenly understanding what was going on. I know what the problem is. I'm falling in love with Keith West!

Seven

"We made it!"

Susan and Chris stood at their lockers, grinning from ear to ear.

"I know!" agreed Susan. "I never thought we'd be able to pull it off. But we did! For a whole day we managed to convince everyone at school that I was Chris and you were Susan!"

"It wasn't easy, though. There were a couple of times there when I thought I was going to give the whole thing away. Like when your art teacher, Mr. Smith, stopped me on my way out of his class and asked me how I was enjoying the book he'd lent me." Chris rolled her eyes and shook her head.

"What did you say?"

"Oh, I raved about it. I went on and on about how much I was getting out of it. I said I'd started reading it Saturday night and I just couldn't put it down. Hey, Sooz, what book was he talking about, anyway?"

Her twin started to giggle. *"Basic Color Theory.*

56

Hardly the kind of thing you'd curl up with in front of a fireplace on a Saturday night!''

"Oh, no! Now Mr. Smith must think I'm really weird!''

"You mean he thinks that *I'm* really weird!'' Susan laughed. "Well, I have to admit that I also had a couple of instances when things were touch and go. Would you please tell me who Carla is?''

"Carla Truscott, of course. She was the captain of the varsity cheerleading team last year. Why?''

"Some girl passed me a note in English class about her. And I didn't know who she was talking about.''

"Really? What did the note say?''

"I don't remember. Something about some guy who had finally asked her out.''

"You're kidding! You mean Jim finally got up the nerve? I don't believe it! I never thought I'd see it happen. When did he ask her? Where are they going? What did Amy say?''

"*Christine*," Susan groaned. "I have no idea! I don't even know who these people are, remember?''

"Oh, yeah. Sorry. I forgot for a minute. I'll just have to ask around and find out for myself.''

"But you're already supposed to know about it. After all, that friend of yours wrote you a note about it.''

"You're right. Oh, dear. Now I'll never find out. I won't be able to ask anybody about it for two whole weeks. I'll *die* of curiosity.''

"Look, I'll do what I can to find out all about it. In the meantime, why don't we walk home together? I want to hear every single detail about your day. I can't wait to find out what Susan Pratt did today.'' While she was too shy to mention it, what she was most anxious to hear about was how Chris had managed with Keith West. Had her more outgoing twin had any more success in catching his attention than she had?

"I want to hear about everything that happened to you today, too, Sooz. But I have some errands to do before I go home. So you'd better go along without me and we can talk later."

"Errands? What kind of errands?"

"Oh, nothing much." Chris shrugged. "I just want to browse around at Mitch's Art Supply Store. See what kind of things they have."

"Okay." Susan suppressed a smile. She could see that her twin was a little embarrassed by her newfound interest in art, so she was careful not to tease her or say anything to discourage her. "I'll see you later on, then."

The two girls sorted through their lockers until they had found the books they needed to do their homework, then traded them with brief explanations about the types of assignments that were usually given.

As Susan started down the sidewalk away from the red brick building, she was lost in thought. She was still trying to digest all the things that had happened to her that day. More important, she was sorting out the surprising facts she had learned about her sister's life.

Gee, I always thought Chris had things so easy, she mused. All the girl friends and boyfriends she wanted, her easygoing personality, being in the center of everything. But there's a price for that popularity. Having to put up with people like Richard Collier, for one thing. She shivered as she remembered how he had acted toward her, putting his arm around her and making disparaging remarks about Susan Pratt.

Then there's the way the teachers treat her. I always assumed that teachers behaved the same way toward everyone. But I found out in English class that they can be as sarcastic and difficult to get along with as anybody else. Poor Chris! No wonder she hates schoolwork so much!

Thinking back, Susan could remember a time when Chris had refused to go to school. Every morning she would cry and fight with her mother and then be dragged off, kicking and screaming, to the school bus. At the time Susan had thought she was merely being childish, acting like a spoiled little kid. But now she understood how hard it must have been for her. She made a vow to start offering her twin help with her homework and to put in a good word for her with her teachers every chance she got.

And then there were the things she had learned about herself that day, about how Susan Pratt was perceived at school. Most of the students seemed to think she was nice enough but that she was so quiet and timid that no one ever got the chance to know her. Why had she never made an attempt to get to know Chris's friends? Whenever they came over to the house, Susan always hid in her room behind closed doors. She told herself she wanted nothing to do with them. But maybe the truth was that she was afraid they wanted nothing to do with her. It was certainly something to think about!

As Susan rounded a corner clutching her schoolbooks to her chest, her mind still a million miles away, she suddenly jumped back in horror. She heard the shrieking of two sets of brakes, then froze as she realized what was about to happen. She braced herself, then watched two cars collide, one running into the front of the other with full force. It was a terrifying sight, and the noise of the brakes, the tires skidding, and the crash of heavy metal against metal hurt her ears.

Then, for a few seconds, there was a dead silence,

broken only by the tinkling sound of shattering glass. Susan immediately sprang into action. She ran over to see if anyone was hurt, her heart pounding so hard she could scarcely breathe.

"Are you all right?" she called as she neared the wreckage. "Is anyone badly hurt?"

The doors of both cars opened, and a man climbed out of each car. One of them was very young, probably a teenager. The other one—the one who had run the stop sign and caused the accident—was an older man, in his fifties or sixties.

"What's the matter with you, boy?" The older man scowled. "What are you trying to do, kill an innocent passenger?"

"*Me?*" cried the young man. "*You're* the one who ran the stop sign on the corner!"

"I don't know what you're talking about," the first man insisted. "Here you are, a wild kid, driving around town like some kind of maniac. . . . You ought to have your driver's license taken away. That is, if you even *have* a license! And good luck to you if you don't have the registration for that vehicle. Hey, that's not a *stolen* car, by any chance, is it?"

It didn't take Susan long to realize that neither of the drivers had noticed her. The older one was so involved in yelling his false accusations that he never bothered to look around. And the younger one was so distressed that he didn't know what to do.

"Gee, now my neck is starting to hurt," the older man went on as Susan drew closer. "I've probably got whiplash. You'll pay for this, young man!"

"Excuse me," Susan said softly, walking up behind them and tapping the boy on the shoulder. "I just saw this whole accident happen. Maybe I can be of some help."

"What?" The older man glared at her. "Who are you? You his girl friend or something?"

"No, sir," Susan replied. "I never met either of you before. But as I said, I saw the accident. I was walking home from school, and just as I turned the corner, the collision took place." She hesitated, watching the older man grow even more angry. "I believe you're mistaken, sir, about the cause of the accident. I saw very distinctly that it was you who ran the stop sign, right over there, on the corner of Juniper and Elm."

A look of relief spread across the boy's face.

"I don't know too much about what you're supposed to do when you have an accident," Susan went on, "but I remember hearing my father say once that the first thing to do is call the police."

"That's right," the boy agreed. "Is there a phone around here? I don't live in this town, so I don't know my way around very well."

"I'll say," the older man mumbled. "Reckless driving . . . kids like you should be put in jail!"

Susan ignored him. "There's a little grocery store right down that side street over there. If you want, I'll run over there and call the police."

"Would you really do that?" The boy looked so grateful that Susan felt like taking his hand and telling him that everything was going to be all right.

"Of course. No trouble at all. I'll just leave my books in your car, if you don't mind." She dropped them onto the backseat through an open window. "I'll be back in five minutes."

Susan trotted down the street toward Gray's Grocery. Meanwhile the two drivers exchanged insurance and registration information. When she returned with the report that the police would be arriving as soon as they could, the two men were standing as far apart as possible, each leaning against his own car and avoiding the other.

"Thanks for calling the police," the boy said when she joined him. "Boy, my father's going to be furious! This is his car. He lent it to me so I could get to basketball practice."

"Where do you live?"

"Over in Pointersville. But our school gym is being renovated, so we've been using the junior high school gym in Whittington. How about you?"

"I live here in Whittington." She paused, not sure whether this was the time and place for making polite small talk. But before she had time to decide, the boy started talking.

"By the way, my name is Jason. Jason Simms. I'm a senior over at Pointersville High. How about you? Are you a senior, too?"

"No, I . . ."

Before she had a chance to answer, a police car rolled up.

"It's about time," the older man grumbled to no one in particular. "I don't have all day to stand around here."

"Okay, what seems to be the problem here?" the policeman asked as he got out of the car, holding a pad and pen. "Why don't you start by each giving me your own version of what happened?"

While the two drivers talked to the police officer and argued between themselves, Susan stepped back, out of the way. She wasn't sure if as a witness it was her duty to stay or if she was just in the way, hanging around while the policeman tried to straighten everything out. Then she saw Jason point in her direction and the officer glance over at her. She stood up straighter as he approached her.

"You the witness?" he asked.

"Yes, sir. I'm the only witness, as far as I know."

"What's your name?" the policeman asked, taking out the pad of paper and clicking his ball-point pen.

"Uh—my name?"

"Yes," he said impatiently. "I'll need your name and address."

Her name. The policeman wanted to know who she was. Susan thought of the Banana Split Affair and the contract she and Chris had drawn up.

No matter what, she had pledged, I'll keep the identity of Christine Pratt.

This was serious business, she knew, but she *was* committed to trading identities with her twin. What should she say? She couldn't think straight. The policeman was watching her with a frown, his pen poised over the accident report form.

"Your name, please, miss?" he repeated.

"Christine Pratt," she blurted out.

Susan immediately regretted having lied. She could feel herself turning red. But she hadn't *meant* to lie; it had just slipped out. And she couldn't very well change her answer now. How would it look if she suddenly said, "No, my name isn't Christine. It's Susan," to the policeman? How would she ever be able to explain that she had lied when she told him her name?

No, she decided, she had better stick to her story. Perhaps she would never be called to testify as a witness. And if she were, maybe she could get Chris—the *real* Chris—to fill in for her.

It was so hard to think straight. Her heart was

pounding again, so hard that she thought she might faint. Besides, it was already too late. The police officer was getting ready to leave. What's done is done, she told herself, wishing she had been able to think more clearly before answering.

The police car finally drove away. Then the older driver left, still scowling and mumbling under his breath. Once she and Jason were left alone, he turned to her and shook her hand.

"Thanks a lot. You really helped me out. With you as a witness, I'll have no trouble proving the accident was the other guy's fault. All that nonsense about whiplash and teenage drivers! I'll be grateful forever."

He smiled then, and Susan noticed for the first time what a good-looking fellow he was. Reddish hair, blue eyes, a friendly, sincere smile that lit up his face. He had an easygoing manner that she was immediately drawn to. "Listen, Chris, I think I should get your phone number."

Susan was tempted to ask, "What for?" But then she remembered that she was playing the role of her sister. "My goodness," she teased, talking in Chris's flirtatious manner, "are you planning to ask me out for a date?"

A look of confusion crossed Jason's face. "Uh, well, I, uh, just figured that if you're the only witness to my car accident and I might need you to testify at a hearing, I should at least know how to contact you."

Susan could feel herself turning as red as the stop sign that the other driver had ignored. "Oh, of course," she stammered, feeling very foolish. Her real self took over then, and all she wanted to do was run away. But she jotted down the name Christine Pratt, along with her address and telephone number, on the piece of paper that Jason handed her.

"Thanks again!" He smiled one of his genuine smiles

again. "I really appreciate your help. Hey, can I give you a lift home, Chris?"

"No, thanks. That's okay. I only live a couple of blocks from here."

The last thing Susan wanted was for Jason to run into her mother and tell her all about what had happened. She was only too aware of the fact that she had made a terrible mistake by pretending she was Chris. But now it was too late. All she could do was hope things didn't get any worse.

"All right, then, Chris. Good-bye! I'll be talking to you!"

You mean you'll be talking to *Susan*, she thought ruefully. You only *think* you'll be talking to Christine.

With a heavy heart and a worried look on her face, Susan watched Jason drive away with his crushed fender, then started on her way home.

Eight

It wasn't until she got home that Susan realized she had left her schoolbooks in Jason's car. And while she had given him her address and telephone number, it had never occurred to her to ask for his.

"Darn!" she said aloud as she paused in her task of setting the table for dinner to wonder how on earth she was going to track him down and get her books back, preferably without anyone in her family knowing about it. Susan cursed herself for behaving in such a typically Susan-ish way. If she hadn't been in such a hurry to get away from the good-looking boy, if she had lingered for a few more minutes to flirt with him the way Chris would have, it might have occurred to her to ask Jason for his address and phone number, too.

But no. She had been in her usual hurry to get away from Jason Simms. Was it really because she was embarrassed about being so flip, asking him if he planned to call her up and ask her out? Or was it simply because she had just begun to notice what an attractive, friendly boy Jason was?

"Darn, oh, darn!" she exclaimed again, this time because of her own stupid shyness as well as the fact that she would have to work out a way to retrieve her books.

Her mother overheard her talking to herself and poked her head in from the kitchen.

"Is something wrong, dear?" Mrs. Pratt had taken to calling her daughters dear and honey rather than using their names. That was because she was never completely sure which twin it was that she was speaking to.

"I'm sorry, Mom. Did you say something to me?"

"Am I imagining things, or did I just hear you say 'Darn!' as you put down that fork? Is there something about forks that distresses you?"

Susan laughed in spite of herself. "I like forks a lot," she joked. "They help feed me. And I love anything that helps me eat."

Susan returned to her table setting, relieved when her mother went back into the kitchen. She was tempted to tell her all about the car accident—and, more important, about how she had given her sister's name to the police and pretended that she was Christine Pratt instead of Susan. But she had decided not to. As much as she wanted to confide in her parents, to have her mother and father assure her that everything would be all right, she knew that the safest thing to do was wait for a while. She had made a stupid mistake, and she wanted to see if there was any way she could fix things up by herself before confessing to her parents how dumb she had acted.

As she placed the last knife next to her sister's plate, the telephone rang in the kitchen. She listened to her mother's voice mumbling intelligibly into the receiver.

"Susan," her mother called in, sticking her head out

of the doorway between the kitchen and the dining room, "it's for you. That is, it's someone who wants to speak to Chris." Mrs. Pratt then diplomatically disappeared into the living room to give her daughter privacy.

"Hello?" Susan said, wondering which of Chris's countless friends and admirers was calling.

"Hi, is this Chris Pratt?"

"Yes. Who is this, please?" Susan didn't recognize the male voice at the other end of the line. But then again, one thing she had learned at school that day was that the circles that she and her twin traveled in were so different that she hardly knew any of the same people as Chris.

"This is Jason. Jason Simms. Remember? The car accident?"

"Of course I remember. It's not every day that I'm the witness to a car crash!"

"Well, I'm certainly glad to hear that! Otherwise I might think you were some kind of jinx or something!" In a more serious tone he said, "You know, you accidentally left your schoolbooks in my car. And there was so much confusion with the police and that terrible man who ran into me that I just drove off with them without even thinking. Anyway, is it okay if I stop by and drop them off?"

"Sure. That'd be great."

"Okay. It's the least I could do for someone who was willing to step forward and bail me out. I've got your address, and I have a general idea of where it is. So I'll come by right after dinner. How about eight o'clock?"

By the time she hung up, Susan's bad mood had lifted. She felt strangely euphoric, as if someone had just told her the best news in the world. She was glad she'd get her books back so promptly and that she didn't have to go through the hassle of tracking Jason down. But more than that, she was excited over the prospect of seeing Jason again.

"You're being silly!" she scolded herself as she ran upstairs to wash her face and comb her hair. "Jason Simms is only interested in you as the witness to his car accident. Nothing more!"

Nevertheless, she put on her makeup with extra care and made sure she doused herself with a light, flowery cologne before he came over.

Susan was fidgety all through dinner.

"What in the world is *wrong* with you, my dear sister?" Chris pretended to complain. "Do you have ants in your pants? You're acting as if you're about to go skydiving for the very first time in your entire life."

"Maybe I am," Susan returned with a mysterious smile. "Or maybe I'm just in a good mood today."

"That reminds me," their father said. "How did it go today? Did you two masters of disguise—or should I say 'mistresses of disguise'?—manage to convince everyone at school that Chris was Susan and Susan was Chris?"

"You bet!" they both exclaimed. The twins began an enthusiastic review of the events of the day, laughing and interrupting each other as they shared both the humorous and the nerve-racking experiences with their parents. Susan, of course, made no mention of Jason Simms, the car accident, or the way in which she had used her sister's name.

When Chris and Susan went into the kitchen together to put the dishes into the sink, Susan said in what she hoped was a casual voice, "Don't forget, sis. Once we're alone, I want to hear all about what happened today in art class."

Chris remained silent. She had intended to repeat every word of the conversation she had had with Keith West to her sister, of course, but now that she was faced with actually having to do it, she felt strange. It was almost as if the time she had spent with him was *special* to her in some way, and to talk about it, to share it with someone else, would be like telling a secret that she had sworn to keep.

But she said, "Oh, sure. Later on, when we're upstairs, doing our homework." She was tempted to hold some of the detail back, as if to tell everything was some sort of betrayal. But that was ridiculous, she knew. After all, Susan had had her eye on Keith West for ages. She deserved to know everything that had gone on. Especially since Chris had been posing as Susan!

Promptly at eight, the doorbell rang. Susan, who had been hanging around in the living room to make sure she would be the one to answer the door, called, "I'll get it!" and quickly flung the door open.

"Hiya, Chris!" Jason grinned.

"Hi, Jason." Once again Susan was taken aback by the warmth and friendliness that he emanated. "Um, you don't mind if I don't ask you in right now, do you? My mother is sick. . . ."

"Oh, no. That's okay. I mainly wanted to get these back to you."

He thrust a pile of books at her, the texts and notebooks that she had forgotten on the backseat of his car.

"Thanks, Jason. I appreciate you driving all the way over here with these."

"To tell you the truth, there was another reason I wanted to talk to you, besides your books."

"Really? What?"

"Well, I've been thinking about what you said before."

"What do you mean?" Susan couldn't remember having said anything out of the ordinary to Jason.

"About me wanting your phone number so I could call you and ask you for a date."

"Oh, that." Susan could feel herself turning red. But then she remembered that she was supposed to be Chris. Confident, flirty Chris. What would she say in a situation like this?

"And you decided it was a terrific idea, right?"

Jason was a little taken aback. But he stuttered, "Well, uh, as a matter of fact, I did! So how about it? Would you like to go out with me Saturday night?"

Susan couldn't believe her ears. Jason was asking her out! Here she had met him only today, and he was so interested in her that he wanted to see her again on Saturday. And she had been convinced he thought she was brash!

Then again, it was really Chris that he wanted to go out with. She would be the one to go out on the date, but she would have to pretend she was her sister. Her bold, teasing sister. Would she be able to pull it off? And would she be disappointed, somewhere in the back of her mind, that it was the outgoing Chris's personality he was attracted to, not the shy, quiet one of Susan, the one she really possessed?

Well, she wasn't about to start worrying about that now. She flashed on her widest smile and, in her most Chris-like manner, exclaimed, "You're on, Jason! I'm already counting the minutes until Saturday night!"

Once again Jason looked a little surprised by the tone of her response. But Susan was so excited over the prospect of dating Jason that she didn't notice. No matter what role she was playing, *she* would be the one to enjoy Jason's company. She was beginning to see just how much fun it was to be popular with boys. At least, with one she liked as much as Jason Simms!

Nine

"Hello again!"

Chris glanced up from the watercolor painting she was working on and found herself face-to-face with Keith West.

"Oh, hi, Keith! I'm sorry I didn't notice you standing there. I got so absorbed in what I was doing . . ."

"So I see." He grinned. "I've been standing here for almost five minutes watching you work."

"You've been watching me work? Whatever for?" Chris was pleased that Keith was taking such a sudden interest. *No, silly!* she reminded herself. *It's Susan he's taking a sudden interest in. And don't you forget it!*

"It's fascinating," replied Keith. "You get so wrapped up in your work, it's as if you've completely forgotten that the rest of the world even exists."

"That's because I'm concentrating so hard." *If he only knew!* Chris couldn't help smiling to herself. *I have to concentrate as hard as I can. That's because I don't know what I'm doing!*

"Well, whatever your secret is, it sure as heck works!"

Keith twisted his head around so he could get a better view of the half-finished painting on Chris's desk. He studied it for a minute, then frowned.

"What exactly are you trying to say here, Susan? This is so different from your usual style that it looks as if somebody else did it."

Chris looked at him sharply. Had he seen through her? Or was he merely making an innocent comment? She answered him cautiously.

"Since this is an experimental project, trying to mix our own colors and all, I decided to try something totally different in terms of my style, too. Don't you like it?"

"Oh, yes!" Keith assured her quickly. "I didn't say it's not as good as your usual stuff. I was just surprised to see that you're so . . . versatile."

Goodness! Chris thought. This Keith really is stuck on Susan! He can find no fault with her, no matter what!

She looked at her painting critically. It was a childlike drawing of a house done in bold strokes of muddy colors. Chris had to admit that no matter how she judged it, it still looked like the first artistic attempt of a five-year-old.

"Yes," Keith went on, "I always liked that primitive style of art. It's so honest, so innocent. You've really managed to capture that effect well."

"Thanks, Keith." Chris smiled at him warmly. "Your opinion means a lot to me."

After an embarrassing pause during which neither Keith nor Chris could think of anything else to say, Keith said, "Well, I guess I should get back to work. This project is due tomorrow, and I still have a lot to do on it. See you around!"

Chris noticed that he started to walk away from her with some reluctance. A sudden sense of urgency tugged at her.

"Hey, Keith, wait a second!"

"Yeah, Susan?"

What am I doing? she thought in horror. For a split second she had let her Chris personality take over. She was about to ask Keith if he wanted to have lunch with her sometime. That was the kind of question Chris asked all the time, once she was certain a boy was interested in her but too shy to do anything about it. And it was exactly the kind of thing that her sister Susan would never ask. After all, she had to keep in mind that it was Susan who was talking to Keith West—shy, timid Susan—and not the confident, bold Chris.

"Oh, uh, never mind. I was just going to ask you, uh, if you knew what kind of project Mr. Smith was going to assign next."

"Nope," he said with a shrug. "Your guess is as good as mine." And he turned away.

Rats! thought Chris, turning back to her painting so she wouldn't be too conspicuous. It's obvious that Keith likes Susan. Or at least *me* as Susan. But he *is* shy. Between his shyness and Susan's shyness, how am I ever going to get them together? How can I possibly get him to ask her out?

Is it Susan you're so concerned with? asked a devilish little voice inside her as she dreamily stirred her cup of cloudy water with her brush. Is it really your twin sister's social life you're so worried about, her long-term crush on Keith West? Or could it possibly be your own that's making you put so much energy into this?

It was a difficult question and one that Chris wasn't quite ready to tackle. So she put Keith West out of her mind and instead focused her thoughts on the dismal piece of artwork that sat before her.

"Three days down, eleven to go!" cried Chris, stretching her legs across the floor of her bedroom, where she was lying on a mass of pillows.

"I'd say we're doing quite well for ourselves, too, all things considered." Susan sat on her twin's bed, legs crossed Indian-style, clutching the faded, threadbare teddy bear that had lived in Chris's room for as long as either of them could remember.

"I'll say! And not only are we having a blast by managing to convince everybody at school that I'm you and you're me, either. Even though I went into this thing just looking for a good time, I'm learning an awful lot about the world. And about you, too, dear twin."

"I know what you mean. With all due respect, I'm finding out the hard way that being Christine Pratt is not all fun and games."

"Odd that you should say that." Chris grinned. "I was just going to say the exact same thing about you."

"That reminds me." Susan weighed her words, not quite sure of how to begin. "I wanted to ask you about Richard Collier."

"Oh, yuck! Mr. Creep-o Sleaze-o himself!"

"Chris! If that's the way you feel, why is he so convinced that you think he's God's gift to women?"

Chris paused to think about her sister's question. "Because I led him to believe I thought he was an okay guy."

"But *why*? I just heard you say that you can't stand him!"

Chris rolled over onto her stomach and rested her chin in her hands. Without meeting her twin's eyes, she said,

"Sooz, let me teach you Lesson One about being popular with the important kids at school. In fact, I'm surprised someone as sharp as you hasn't already figured this out. When you make an effort to be accepted, sometimes you have to do things you don't want to do. Go places you don't want to go to—maybe even places you're afraid to go—just because all the other kids are going. Do things you don't exactly feel terrific about. And be nice to people you can't stand, just because they have some kind of power within that group."

"Richard Collier is considered powerful? I can't imagine why. Do your friends really like him?"

Chris shook her head. "No, not really. To tell you the truth, most of them can't stand him. They put up with him and humor him and let him belong, the way I do."

"But what on earth *for*? If no one can stand him, then why do they go out of their way . . ."

"Because his older brother owns a liquor store, that's why." Chris sighed, sounding as if she were getting impatient with her sister's questions. But the reality was that she hated talking about this. She hated the fact that even though she knew what she was telling Susan was horribly wrong, she had accepted it just to fit in with the rest of her crowd.

"I'm afraid I still don't understand. . . ."

"Look. The kids I hang around with have parties a lot, and the main purpose is for everybody to get drunk. They think it's cool or something. They like to pretend they're grown-up." Chris grimaced. "Grown-up! What usually ends up happening is that the boys go outside and fight with each other and the girls throw up all over their pretty party clothes. The boys go home with black eyes and the girls go home crying. And the next day everybody calls up everybody else and starts carrying on about the terrific time they had."

"I've never seen you do that. I mean you usually come home early. And in pretty good shape, too."

"I know. That's because I never really drink. I pretend to, that's all. I carry around a glass of Coke all night, and whenever someone asks me what I'm drinking, I make a big deal about how drunk I am."

"But *why*, Chris?" Susan's voice was tight. "Why put yourself through all that? People you don't like, like Richard, and pretending to get drunk and watching all your friends get sick or start fistfights . . ."

"You've seen for yourself how great it is to *belong*. To walk down the corridors at school and have everybody know you. Have everybody *like* you. The class president, all the captains of all the teams . . . Don't you see, Susan? It makes me important!"

"You mean it makes you *feel* important," her sister returned in a scolding tone. "There's a big difference there. If that's what you have to do to be accepted by those kids, I think I'd rather go back to being a nobody."

"That's a choice everybody has to make. You do what you want. As for me, I still think it's worth it to go along with a few things that I'm not crazy about to reap all the benefits of being popular."

Even as she said those words, Chris could hear her voice wavering with uncertainty. Keith West's face popped into her mind, smiling that shy, funny smile, his cheeks tinted pink as he talked to her. *There* was someone who didn't run with her crowd yet was perfectly nice. *More* than nice. Maybe even a little bit special.

She realized that there was a dreamy smile on her face, and she immediately snapped back to reality.

"That reminds me. I have something else to report on Keith West."

"Oh, really?" Susan chirped, leaning forward and hugging her sister's teddy bear even tighter. "What happened? What did you say? What did *he* say?"

"Hold on! Let me catch my breath!" Chris repeated the brief conversation she had had with Keith that day in art class. The two girls laughed over his comment about her ability to capture the essence of primitive art, shrieking hysterically until they had to hold their stomachs so they wouldn't feel as if they were about to burst open.

"If he only knew!" Chris cried, gasping and rolling on the floor. "Primitive! If he only knew how primitive I really was! The reason I paint like a kid is because I was six years old the last time I held a paintbrush in my hand!"

"Ladies! Ladies!" The sound of their mother's voice and her sudden appearance in the doorway of Chris's bedroom calmed them down. "Can you two stop laughing like wild hyenas long enough for your poor mother to deliver a message?"

The twins covered their mouths to keep from giggling.

"Sorry, Mom," said Susan. "We didn't realize you were there. I'm afraid we got a little carried away."

"That's the understatement of the year! I hate to interrupt all this girlish glee, but there's a telephone call for Susan."

The girls exchanged glances. "I guess I should get that," Chris said, wriggling to a standing position and starting for the door. "Who is it?"

"I don't know. One of you women's countless admirers. I didn't ask his name. I can't keep them straight anyway."

The real Susan was growing increasingly interested. "Well, go find out, for heaven's sake! I'm dying to know who's calling me!"

"You'll be the very first to know," Chris called over her shoulder, running to the phone.

"Hello?" she said softly, turning on her Susan personality.

"Hi, Susan?" The caller cleared his throat as if he were very, very nervous. Chris still couldn't recognize his voice. "This is, uh, Keith. You know, Keith West? From Mr. Smith's art class?"

"Keith! How nice to hear from you!" There, that sounded like the kind of thing Susan would say, didn't it? "How are you?"

"I'm fine. How about you?"

"Fine, thanks."

There was a long, painful pause. Is this why he called? Chris thought impatiently. To ask how I was? To ask how *Susan* was?

"Well, uh, I guess you wonder why I'm calling."

Another pause. This time Chris was more understanding. After all, this was Keith West, the boy she had admired for his gentleness and shyness that was somehow charming. He wasn't one of the brash boys she usually went out with. Besides, she assumed he had called her merely to ask a question about the art class assignment or something else related to school. So when he blurted out his next question, she was shocked.

"Susan, would you like to go out with me this weekend?"

Chris could feel how difficult it was for him to ask a girl out. He must have really like her—or Susan, or whoever he thought he was talking to—to get up the courage to call. Chris had heard dozens of boys ask her that same question, yet never had she been so flattered.

"I'd love to, Keith! Where would you like to go?"

"Terrific!" He sounded surprised and relieved. Even grateful. "There's a new movie at the Kensington that sounds pretty good. I thought we could go there." Then he added, "You haven't seen it, have you?"

"To be perfectly honest, Keith, I haven't been to a movie in ages," Chris lied. "It sounds like fun."

"Okay! How about Saturday night? I'll come by for you about seven-thirty."

"Great."

Another long pause.

"Well, okay then, Susan. See you then. Oh, yeah, I'll see you in art class tomorrow, too."

"Right. Keith?"

"Yeah?"

"Thanks for calling. I'm really looking forward to this weekend." That was a very Chris thing to say, but this time she meant it. She really, really meant it.

"Yeah, me, too. 'Bye!"

Well, how do you like that? Chris thought triumphantly, continuing to stare at the phone long after she had hung up. *I actually got bashful Keith West to ask Susan out.*

As she hurried back to her bedroom to tell her sister the good news, she felt torn. She was happy for her sister, because after the two weeks of the Banana Split Affair were over, she would still be going out with Keith. But she felt a twinge of regret, too. Here she had managed to match her twin up with the boy *she* had developed a crush on! How could she possibly be expected to feel good about that?

Oh, I wish I were Chris again, she moaned to herself.
. . . I want to go back to being myself!

But then you never would have even met Keith West!
another voice inside reminded her.

Now I don't know how to feel! she thought mourn-
fully. But as far as her sister was concerned, she was
determined to act happy for her. After all, it was Susan
who had been interested in Keith first and for a long
time, besides. So she swallowed hard and put on her
biggest, most sincere smile.

"Susan!" she cried, waltzing into her bedroom, where
her twin sat waiting. "You'll never guess who that was!"

Ten

Susan sat stiffly in the front seat of the car, her hands folded in her lap, her eyes directed straight ahead. As the car swerved around a corner at seventy miles per hour, just missing a trash can, she closed her eyes and counted to ten. Counting sometimes had a calming effect on her, but that night even that had lost its magical powers.

I wish I were anywhere but here, she thought. How did I ever let myself get into this?

Aloud, she said in what she hoped was a nonjudgmental, conversational tone of voice, "Gee, Richard, do you think maybe you could slow down just a little bit? I don't want to be the first one to arrive at Slade's party."

Richard Collier cast her a sidelong glance. "Relax, Chris. What's the matter with you tonight? You seem awfully uptight."

"Who, me?" Susan tossed her head in what she hoped was a devil-may-care, Christine-like way. "I'm fine. It's you who's acting strange. What's with the wild man act all of a sudden?"

"Hey, come on, Babes. You know I have to get to Slade's before the other kids. Got to check on the booze supply. Make sure there's enough to go around, you know?"

I'm sure there will be, Susan thought with chagrin. From what Chris told me about these parties, it sounds as if not having enough liquor is the least of their problems.

Susan remained silent for the rest of the ride to Slade's. A tight knot had formed in her stomach that made it impossible for her to make pleasant conversation with Richard, whom she was finding increasingly boorish the more time she spent with him. Agreeing to go to Slade's party with him had been Chris's idea.

"Of course you have to go! In the first place, it'll look funny if Chris Pratt doesn't show up. I'm a regular at those parties.

"And in the second place, the whole idea of the Banana Split Affair is for us to see what it's really like to be the other twin. If you start choosing where you want to go and what you want to do, that defeats the whole purpose of the experiment!"

Chris was right, she supposed. But still, if she had known she would have to go on a date with Richard Collier—and to a wild party, no less, where she didn't know a single soul and absolutely anything could happen—she wondered if she would have been so eager to change places with her twin.

Then again, an evening like this did manage to impress upon her that her sister's life was not as glamorous as she had always imagined. Chris didn't like Richard Collier any better than she did, and she thought the idea of having parties at kids' houses where their parents weren't home and getting so drunk they couldn't handle themselves was ridiculous and childish. Yet she did it all the time, because it was part of the price she had to pay for her popularity.

Popularity! Susan thought scornfully. Now that I know a little bit more about what it's all about, I realize that I'd much rather stay at home on weekend nights and paint or read a good book!

True to Richard's prediction, they were the first to arrive at Slade's house. Slade, she discovered, was a senior at Pointersville High. When she learned that, she became excited.

"Do you happen to know a student at Pointersville named Jason Simms? He's a senior, too," she asked him eagerly as she emptied countless ice trays into a big bowl that was to serve as an ice bucket. She and Slade's girl friend, who had also been a student at Pointersville before she dropped out to take a job as a receptionist at a small factory, had immediately been sent to the kitchen to get things ready for the party. Slade and Richard, meanwhile, carried carton after carton from the garage.

"Yeah, I've seen him around," Slade answered without much interest. "Why? That creep isn't a friend of yours, is he?"

"Oh, no," Susan assured him quickly. "I just . . . ran into him once. The only reason I even mentioned him is that he's the only person I know at Pointersville."

"Well, you know *us* now!" giggled Shelley, Slade's girl friend.

"Yeah, but you're not in school anymore," Slade commented with disdain before disappearing back into the garage. Susan was surprised by his attitude toward her, but Shelley seemed not to notice. She continued stacking glasses, humming a tuneless melody.

This is going to be a long night, Susan thought with a sigh. I have a feeling that no matter how hard I try to mix with these people, I really have very little in common with them. I guess being liked by a lot of people simply isn't as important to me as it is to Chris. Hanging around with a bunch of people you don't even like seems like an awful waste of time to me, even if the payoff is having every important kid at school wave at you in the corridors.

Susan was relieved when the other party guests started to arrive. Once the living room was full of people, it would be that much easier for her to hide. She recognized more faces than she had expected, simply because these were the juniors and seniors whom *everyone* knew. Team captains, club presidents, student officers, class clowns. One thing was certain: Whether she was able to recognize them or not, they all knew who she was. Chris Pratt was better known around school than Susan had ever expected. But instead of feeling flattered or important when everyone greeted her by her name and a few words of small talk, she felt as if she were living in a small town where everyone knew everything about her that there was to know. Not only were there no *new* people for Chris to meet at these parties; there was little room for privacy.

Or individuality. One of the first things Susan noticed as flocks of kids came into Slade's living room laughing and chattering and ready to have a good time was that everyone dressed the same, wore their hair the same, and used the same expressions as everybody else. It was as if some unacknowledged standard existed and to stray very far away from it was unthinkable. Fortunately, Chris had taken extra care in advising her on what to wear that night. Otherwise Susan would have felt extremely out of place.

Once people started arriving regularly, someone turned on a stereo. The sound was so loud that it was impossible to talk to anyone. That was just fine with Susan. She grabbed a handful of pretzels and leaned against a chair, hoping no one would notice her.

"Hey, Chris, how 'bout a dance?" Richard came in from the kitchen. His crooked grin and flushed cheeks gave away the fact that he had already started drinking. As he leaned close to her and grabbed her hands, there was no doubt in Susan's mind. Richard's breath reeked of alcohol.

"Not right now, thanks," she yelled over the noise. "I think I'll just watch everybody else for a while."

"Aw, don't be such a wet blanket." Refusing to take no for an answer, Richard pulled her away from the safety of her chair and dragged her out to the center of the dance floor. Then she had no choice but to start moving to the music, copying what all the others were doing.

It wasn't long before Richard leaned over and said, "Hey, hey, little girl! Ready for a drink yet?"

Susan's immediate reaction was to say, "No, thanks." But she remembered her sister's technique of pretending to get drunk along with all the other kids. She felt stupid, but there was no other way out. Not unless she wanted to start an argument with Richard. And Chris would never forgive her if she started giving her friends a hard time while she was playing the Chris role.

So she smiled at Richard flirtatiously and said, "Sure. I thought you'd never ask!"

"I like your style." He grinned back at her. "What would you like me to get you?"

"Oh, uh . . ." Susan stopped dancing for a few seconds until she could think of an answer. "Don't you bother now. Why don't you find some cute girl to dance with and I'll go browse around the kitchen on my own and see what I can find."

"Okay. If you insist." Before she had a chance to say another word, Richard had run off the dance floor to retrieve one of the other girls in their class.

Nothing like loyalty, thought Susan as she made her way through the crowd of gyrating dancers. But it's just as well. Maybe I've even managed to dump Richard for the rest of the evening.

She ran into Shelley in the kitchen once again. This time she was rinsing out glasses in the sink. Susan was relieved to see a friendly face. While Slade's girl friend was not the kind of girl whose company she would ordinarily seek out, she seemed much kinder than many of the other kids at the party. Or maybe she was just working too hard to have time to act stuck-up.

"Hi, Shelley."

"Oh, hi, Chris. Would you like something to drink? I've sort of been made unofficial bartender."

"Just a Coke, please." Susan was afraid that Shelley would give her a hard time about not drinking liquor, but she simply nodded and got a bottle out of the refrigerator.

"Thanks, Shelley." Susan accepted the glass from her. "Gee, aren't you even going to get a chance to go out to the party and have a good time?"

Shelley laughed softly and went back to washing dishes. "I'm afraid I'm not much for parties. Not this kind, anyway. Oh, Slade likes to get drunk in front of all his friends and show off. But I don't even know these people. I'm just as happy to hide here in the kitchen and get some of the work done."

Susan was surprised at how gentle and sweet Shelley was. She even looked soft and vulnerable, with her plump arms and pale wavy hair.

"Shelley," Susan asked cautiously, leaning against the kitchen counter and staring into her glass of Coke, "please don't take this the wrong way, but doesn't it bother you to hang out with a bunch of kids you have nothing in common with?"

Shelley laughed again and shrugged. "Oh, I don't know. It's what Slade wants. I just go along."

For a minute Susan felt sorry for the fair baby-faced girl up to her elbows in dirty dishwater. But then she realized that what she was doing—and what Chris was doing—was the exact same thing. Just going along rather than making waves to please somebody else. In Shelley's case, it was her boyfriend. In Chris's case, it was a bunch of kids whom she called her friends. Some of them were nice enough, but some of them, like Richard Collier and some of the others who said hello to her in the hall at school but seemed to have no time for her at a party like this, were not even worth talking to.

But Chris had managed to accept that that was just a part of life. And now it turned out that this girl, Shelley, felt the same way.

Maybe it's me, thought Susan with a frown. Maybe I'm the one who's so hard to get along with. Maybe I really am some kind of misfit.

She decided to give Richard Collier another chance. Maybe he wasn't so bad after all. It was possible that no one had ever taken the time to talk to him, to find out what he was really thinking about. She said good-bye to Shelley, then went back into the living room, determined to make a real effort getting to know Richard better.

Susan found him dancing with one of the sophomore

girls on the school's drill team, an exceptionally pretty girl with a perky nose and waist-length blond hair. He was acting as if he had had a few more drinks. Undaunted, Susan went over to him and tapped him on the shoulder.

"Oh, hiya, Babes. Want to cut in?" he leered at her. The blond girl ignored her and just went on dancing.

"Not exactly." She smiled at him pleasantly. "I was wondering if you and I could go someplace a little quieter and talk."

"Talk? What about? There's nothing wrong, is there?"

"Oh, no. Of course not. To tell you the truth, I was just thinking how little we really know about each other. I decided it would be nice if you and I spent some time getting to know each other better."

"Sure!" Richard's face lit up. "Anything you say, Babes!"

As Richard followed her off the dance floor, leaving behind an indignant girl standing with her hands on her hips, Susan called over her shoulder, "Why don't we find a place to sit down in the dining room? It's much quieter there."

"I have a better idea. How about my car?"

"Your car?" she asked, uncertain.

"Sure. It's quiet and pretty warm and it'll give us a chance to get to know each other better without a bunch of nosy kids bothering us." He grinned at her in a funny way, draping his arm around her shoulders the way he had in school that first day of the switch.

"Oh. I guess you're right. Okay."

A few minutes later Susan found herself in the backseat of Richard's car. Her hands were thrust in her pockets to keep them from getting cold. Richard kept looking at her expectantly, as if he were waiting for her to say something.

"So, Richard, tell me: What kinds of things do you like to do when you're not in school?"

"Oh, I don't know. Just hang around, I guess. Hey, are your hands cold?"

"A little. I'm okay. I mean do you like to read or watch TV or play sports? . . ."

"It's silly to keep them in your pockets when I've got two hands that are perfectly warm. And a lot bigger than yours."

He reached for her hands and pulled them out of her pockets. He then held them in his. Susan felt funny, but she supposed she was being silly, just making a big deal about nothing. After all, she had made it obvious her hands were cold. Richard was only trying to be helpful. Wasn't he?

"So, anyway, Richard, what do you like? . . ."

"You know, Chris, I sure don't know why you're being so friendly all of a sudden. For as long as I've known you, you've hardly bothered to give me the time of day. And you've always known how special I think you are. Boy, I don't know what's going on, but whatever helped you decide that you want to know me better sure is a good deal for me!"

Before Susan was even aware of what was going to happen, Richard wrapped his arms around her and started kissing her. It took her a few seconds to regain her composure.

"Richard! Stop it! What do you think you're doing?" Susan pushed him away as hard as she could.

Richard's expression was a combination of surprise and anger. "Hey, what's going on here, Chris? You playing games with me? Here you give me this big come-on about how you want to get to know me better . . ."

"But I *did*! I mean, I *do*!"

"So what did you think we were going to do?"

Susan became so flustered she could hardly speak. "I thought we were going to *talk* to each other! You know, spend some time finding out what kinds of things we like and don't like . . . things like that."

"Boy, Chris, did you ever miss the boat." Richard shook his head, looking over at her as if she were some kind of silly child who had just made a mistake.

Susan was tempted to tell him off, to say what kind of person he was. She didn't often do that kind of thing, but then again, she didn't often get as furious as she was at that particular moment. But just in time, she remembered that she was supposed to be Chris, not Susan. As angry as she was, she had no right to get mad at one of Chris's friends. So instead, she gritted her teeth and said, "Richard, since we're already in your car, why don't you drive me home?"

"What? And miss some of the party?"

Susan glared at him and sighed. "Good gosh, Richard! It's the very least you could do! After all, you *did* bring me here!"

"All right, all right." He scowled. He got the keys out of his pocket and turned on the ignition.

They both remained silent for the entire ride home. It was all Susan could do to mutter a polite "Good-night, Richard. And thanks for the ride!" before jumping out of his car when it pulled up in front of her house.

Susan immediately ran upstairs to Chris's room. Her twin was lying on her bed daydreaming and listening to the radio. As she heard her sister bounding up the stairs, she called, "Susan! How'd it go? Aren't you home a little early?"

"Not early enough! Chris, how could you *do* that to me? How could you send me out to a crazy party like that with that horrible Richard?"

"Susan! What happened? You look as if you're about to start crying! Here, sit down and tell me everything. And calm down! I'll never be able to understand if you don't relax."

Susan sat down on the edge of her sister's bed and told her the whole story. All about how uncomfortable she had felt at the party, how she had felt that what she was doing was no different from what poor Shelley was doing, hiding in the kitchen and doing all the work for the party, how Richard had purposely "misunderstood" what she had said to him about getting to know him better.

"It was a terrible experience!" she moaned when she had finished. "The whole thing was horrible, from start to finish. How could you let that happen to me?"

Chris put her arm around her twin sympathetically. "I'm sorry you had such a rough time," she said, her voice nearly a whisper. "I told you those parties were dreadful. And what happened with Richard . . . Well, you can be sure I'll take care of him, all right, just as soon as I go back to being Chris!" She hugged her sister. "Why didn't you just slug him, Sooz? And you could have given him one for me, too!"

Susan laughed in spite of herself. Somehow she couldn't imagine hitting Richard Collier. Although the more she thought about it, the more she regretted not having thought of it sooner.

"Oh, Chris, I didn't want to do anything to get your friends mad at you. I didn't think I had the right."

"I know. And I appreciate your being so honorable. But next time—if there ever is a next time—feel free to act on what you really feel. Oooh, I can't wait until I'm Chris again!"

The two girls leaned back against the wall, relaxed and in much better humor. "Boy, Chris, I don't know how you do it. There's something to be said for being a wallflower."

"You're no wallflower," Chris assured her. "Let's just say you're a bit more discriminating than I am. Maybe a bit smarter, too."

"Well," Susan sighed. "What's done is done. All I can do is hope that nothing like that ever happens to me again."

"And all I can do is hope that I'm open enough to learn something from all this. But right now, why don't you and I go downstairs and stuff ourselves? I'm pretty sure I noticed a half gallon of chocolate almond chip ice cream in the freezer."

"Ummm." Susan licked her lips. "Sounds like just what I need. It's not a banana split, of course, but it won't be long now. . . ."

"Oh, you!" Her twin sister swatted at her playfully. "As I recall, our agreement was that if we manage to carry this off, you buy me one. And if we don't, I'm the buyer. How do you feel about that arrangement now?"

"I'd better start saving my pennies!" Susan laughed. "Come on. Race you down to the kitchen!"

Eleven

It didn't take Susan long to recover from her traumatic evening with Richard and Slade and the rest of Chris's friends. Especially with her Saturday-night date with Jason growing closer and closer.

"I'm really looking foward to tonight," she confided to her sister as the two of them stood side by side in front of the bathroom mirror after dinner, getting ready for their dates. It was also Chris's night to go out with Keith. And although she didn't dare tell her twin, she, too, was looking forward to the evening with unusual excitement.

"Well, you certainly deserve a good time after last night." Chris leaned forward and peered into the mirror, carefully drawing a comb through the middle of her head to make the center part her sister always wore. "But don't forget that you're supposed to be me. That means no shyness, no talking about books or art or school. Try to act the way I would on a date with a guy I really liked!"

"I will. I mean, I'll try." Susan scrutinized the eye

makeup she had just applied. It was much heavier than what she would have ever considered acceptable but an exact duplicate of the way Chris always wore hers.

When she was certain she looked like a carbon copy of Chris Pratt, including her hair, makeup, and clothes, she surveyed her reflection one more time.

"I guess that's it." She sighed. "I'm ready."

"You look great. Nervous?"

"A little."

"Sooz, that's *you* speaking, not Chris!"

"Don't tell me *you're* not even a little bit nervous!"

Chris paused, then said, "To tell you the truth, I'm scared stiff! It's not going to be any easier for me to pretend I'm you with a . . . a date than it will be for you!"

Chris bit her lip. She had almost said, "With a guy I'm crazy about." But she had remembered just in time that Keith West was supposed to be her sister's crush, not hers. Fortunately, she had managed to catch herself.

"I guess I'll go downstairs and wait," said Susan. "No use hanging around up here, watching you turn yourself into me. Good luck tonight. And have fun, if you can."

"Yeah, you too."

Susan was relieved that Jason arrived on time. The longer she had to wait for something she was apprehensive about, the more nervous she would become. But once he appeared at the front door and smiled at her in a way that made her feel very special, she began to relax. Even though she would be playing the role of Chris Pratt all evening, she really liked Jason. The reality of going out with him—no matter what personality she happened to be wearing—finally struck her. This was nothing to worry about! As a matter of fact, it was going to be fun!

"Hi, Chris! All ready?"

"Hello, Jason. Yes, I'm all set. Shall we go?"

Jason hesitated. "Uh, wait a minute. Don't you want me to make an appearance before your parents? You know, so they can look me over and be sure their daughter isn't going out with one of Hell's Angels?"

"Oh. Well." Susan tried desperately to think of an excuse. Then she remembered that she was Chris. "Oh, don't worry about my folks. They pretty much let me come and go as I please. They trust my judgment."

"Okay. Anything you say."

Once Susan was settled in the front seat of Jason's car, she asked, "So how is this buggy? It looks like it's still running all right."

"The fender's still smashed up. My dad and I spent some time hammering out the dents, but it's still got a long way to go. We'll have to let the pros take care of the rest, but not until the insurance money comes through. First of all, we've got to get the issue of whose fault the accident was cleared up."

"Oh, yeah. Have you heard from that nasty man? The one who caused the collision?"

"My father called him. He's not budging, either. He still insists that I'm the one who was at fault. Of course, I explained the whole thing to my father, and he believes my side of the story." He looked over at Susan and grinned. "The fact that I have a witness helped convince him, too."

Susan swallowed hard and looked out the window. "Oh, right. Do you know anything more about when I'll have to appear at a hearing?"

"No, not yet. In fact you might not have to go through with all that after all. It depends on what happens with the insurance company and all that."

Thank goodness! Susan thought. Now that she didn't have to worry about that so much, she could concentrate on having a good time with Jason. And acting like Chris.

"I hope I don't have to appear," she said flippantly. "To be perfectly honest, I haven't the slightest idea of what one is supposed to wear to a hearing! I don't think I have anything appropriate to wear!"

Once again Jason glanced over at her. But this time the look he wore was one of bewilderment. "Gee, Chris," he said gently. "You sure do say the most peculiar things sometimes."

"Oh, that's just my zany sense of humor," Susan retorted with a wave of her hand. "You know me. I'm hardly ever serious. I'm much too busy having fun."

"Um," was all that Jason said.

"So, where are we going?" Susan asked after the silence that fell between them had become awkward.

"There's a new movie downtown that's supposed to be good. Some of my friends saw it last week, and they said it was worth seeing. That is, if it's okay with you."

"Sure," Susan said flirtatiously. "I always enjoy sitting in the dark with a good-looking boy."

She regretted her comment as soon as she had said it. What a thing to say! And to someone she barely even knew yet! What was wrong with her?

That's how Chris would act, isn't it? another voice said in her defense.

Still, she couldn't be sure. Whenever Chris said smart-alecky things, the boys seemed to love it. Jason, however, seemed made uncomfortable by her playful remarks. Perhaps she was overdoing it a bit . . .

Jason said nothing about her comment. But Susan noticed that he clutched the steering wheel much more tightly than necessary and his lips were drawn into a straight little line.

"Here we are," he said with forced cheerfulness as they pulled into the movie theater's parking lot. "Just in time, too. Look: Everyone's just going in. If we hurry, we can get a good seat."

Susan was about to say something about how she wouldn't mind sitting in the back row with him, but she stopped herself in time. She could see that Jason had had enough of Chris-style cute remarks for now.

When they were settled inside, sitting in the center of the movie theater, Susan decided to make use of the five minutes or so before the film started.

"You know, Jason, I'm *so* glad you picked this movie. I read somewhere that it was filmed in France, and I simply *adore* France. It's such a *civilized* country. And French is such a *gorgeous* language. It sounds more like music than words. And the people—why, they're *divine*! Just divine!"

She was talking so loudly that everyone seated around them could hear her.

In an especially soft voice, Jason said, "Really, Chris? I had no idea you spent time in France. Where did you go?"

"Oh. Well." Susan could feel herself turning red. "I've, uh, never actually *gone* to France. But I've seen a lot of pictures of Paris! And read some things, too! That's almost as good as being there. . . ."

Fortunately the lights went dim at that point and the movie came on. Susan sat in the dark, on the verge of tears. What was *wrong* with her? She was supposed to be acting like Chris, but was this the way she really behaved around boys? Susan always thought she did. But somehow her flirtatiousness had a different effect on the boys she was trying to impress. Susan knew she was doing something wrong—something *very* wrong—but she was doing her best. What was going on?

It was impossible for her to enjoy the movie. It looked as if it were funny; everyone in the theater was laughing except for her. But she couldn't get lost in it. Instead she went over the things she had said in her mind.

Well, she concluded as the movie drew to a close, now I'll get a second chance. Surely Jason will suggest that we go someplace for something to eat. Then I can try toning things down a bit. I'll still act like Chris, but I won't be quite as extreme.

But after she and Jason briefly discussed the movie and climbed back into his car, he said, "Gee, Chris, that ran longer than I expected. I'm afraid I'll have to take you home now. My father asked me to bring the car back early tonight. . . ."

"Oh, that's too bad," Susan said, really meaning it. "I was hoping we'd get a chance to talk some more. I don't feel like we had much of a chance to find out very much about each other."

"Maybe next time."

"Right. Maybe next time," Susan repeated morosely.

Don't cry. Not now, anyway. Wait until you get home. *Chris* would never cry in front of a boy. Not over something like *this*.

Susan was quiet as Jason drove her home. He turned the radio on softly, then started to talk, just for the sake of filling the silence. He talked about his school, the sports he was involved in, his family. He really was a likeable guy, Susan noted. It was too bad.

"Maybe next time," he had said. But Susan knew as he stopped in front of her house that there would never be a "next time."

"I don't suppose you'd like to come in," she offered in a dull voice.

"Gee, thanks, but I really don't have much time. . . ."

Susan decided to give it one more try. I dedicate this remark to my twin sister, she thought halfheartedly.

"Would you like to kiss me good-night, Jason?" She had tried to sound coy, but instead her words sounded silly.

Jason was obviously taken aback. "What? Oh. Gee, Chris, I don't think . . . ."

Before he could finish his sentence, Susan opened the door and flew out of the car. Her eyes were so filled with tears that she could hardly see.

I have to get away, she thought over and over, have to get away . . .

When she reached the living room, she slammed the front door and let the tears that had been building up inside her all night flow freely.

"Is that you, Chris? Or is it Susan?" her mother's voice called from the kitchen. "Whoever it is, what are you doing home so early? Is this some new self-imposed curfew?"

Susan knew if she answered her mother, her voice would crack and betray how upset she was. So she ran upstairs to the safety of her bedroom. She flung herself across her bed and cried into her pillow.

Why? she asked herself over and over again. Why had she acted so foolish? She really liked Jason, more than any boy she had ever met before. And now she had ruined everything. She had behaved stupidly, and now he would never want to see her again. He had certainly made that clear enough. Oh, why did everything have to be so difficult? And why did she have to meet Jason while she and Chris were playing this dumb game of the Banana Split Affair?

Susan couldn't wait until Chris came home. She wanted to tell her everything, to share with her the horror of the evening she had just spent. Maybe talking it over with her would somehow make her feel better. And maybe Chris would have some idea of what she could do to make Jason like her again.

In the meantime, though, all Susan wanted to do was be left alone to cry. She was glad that her mother didn't come looking for her. She must have sensed that something was wrong.

Once I talk to Chris, everything will be all right again, Susan told herself. Chris will know what to do. She always knows how to fix things like this. After all, she's one of the most popular girls at school, isn't she? She must know something about making people like her.

With that comforting thought, Susan stopped crying. Within a few minutes, she had drifted off to sleep.

Twelve

While Susan was sitting in the darkened movie theater with Jason Simms, feeling morose and on the verge of tears, Chris was having one of her most pleasurable dates ever. Her initial perceptions of Keith West were proving to be correct. While he was generally quiet and withdrawn, there was another side of his personality that he showed to those who took the time to get to know him. He was thoughtful, gentle, and had a dry sense of humor that Chris found delightful.

"Where would you like to go?" she asked him when he arrived at the front door of the Pratts.

"I'd *like* to go to Acapulco for three days of snorkeling and sunbathing. But I'm afraid you and I will just have to settle for an evening of roller skating. That is," he added quickly, "if that's all right with you. I know there are some people who end up spending more time sitting down than standing up when they go skating. If you happen to be one of those, we could always find something else to do. I *did* ask you on the phone to see that movie at the Kensington."

"Oh, no," Chris-as-Susan assured him. "Roller skating sounds great. I love skating." As for the *real* Susan, she thought, the very first—and last—time she tried roller skating, she broke her wrist. Isn't it funny how things work out sometimes!

"Okay, then, skating it is. Unfortunately, my limousine is being repaired, so we'll have to take the bus."

"No problem at all. In fact," Chris said in the same dead-serious voice, "I'm kind of tired of running around town in limousines. It'll be nice to try something different, for a change. See how the other half lives."

Chris could tell that both her parents approved of Keith when she introduced him. He shook hands with them both and asked her father what time he wanted his daughter home.

"Boy," Chris teased as they left the house, "you sure are smooth when it comes to getting over the hurdle of parents." She realized immediately that that was a very Chris thing to say.

"What do you mean?" Keith glanced at her quizzically. "I wasn't trying to fool your parents. I was only being polite. No different from the way I act around everyone's parents. I think they deserve some respect, don't you?"

"Of course. I was only kidding."

You'd better watch what you say, Chris scolded herself. Don't forget that you're supposed to be Susan. Besides, Keith isn't the kind of boy who likes to be teased. He's much more serious and sincere than most of the other guys I've gone out with. Whether I'm Chris or Susan in the future, I'd better cool it.

Chris or Susan. She was hit with a flash of guilt. She was supposed to be going out with Keith to make him like her sister, not her. Yet she was having such a hard time remembering that! Goodness, what was she going to do when their second week of the Banana Split Affair was over? Just forget all about Keith and hand him over to Susan? How was she expected to stop herself from liking him?

Well, don't spend your whole evening worrying about that, she told herself. Just have a good time, for whatever it's worth. This may be the first and only time you get to go out with Keith, so at least enjoy it. Worry about the future tomorrow.

"So tell me, Susan," Keith said as they rode the bus to the skating rink. "How did you first get interested in art?"

Chris tried to remember how Susan had gotten involved. "Oh, you know how little kids are always given crayons and paints and all that from kindergarten on. I just happened to like doing drawings and paintings much more than most of the other kids. And from the beginning, my teachers were always saying that I had a lot of talent." Was that too boastful? Chris wondered. Would Susan be so open about complimenting herself? She peeked over at Keith to see how he was reacting. He was simply nodding in agreement, so she decided she was doing all right.

"That's lucky," he said. "It's nice when the things you like to do and the things you're good at are one and the same."

"Well, you're that way, too." Chris could remember Susan saying that she thought Keith was one of the best art students in the school.

"Yeah, but that's not what I want to do in the long run. I hope to become a doctor."

"Really? How exciting! How come?"

"I find science much more interesting than art. Oh, art is fun, of course, and there's a lot to get out of it, both doing it and appreciating it. But I want to help people in a much more concrete way." He turned red at that point, acting more like the bashful Keith Chris knew from art class. "You know, Susan, I've never told anyone that before . . . that I wanted to be a doctor."

"Really? I'm surprised. That's such an impressive career to want to follow."

Keith shrugged. "I guess so. But I'm always afraid people will laugh at me."

"Why? Why should anyone laugh at you?"

"Gee, that's a good question. I guess in reality no one would. But it's just something I worry about sometimes."

"Yeah, me, too." There. That sounded like something Susan would say. Chris tended to go ahead and do whatever she wanted, barging through her life like a bull in a china shop, not stopping to see if any damage had been done until afterward. But Susan was cautious and very much concerned with what other people would think of her.

"Can I ask you something, then, Keith?"

"Sure."

"Why did you tell me, then?"

He hesitated, his cheeks turning pink once again. "I don't know, Susan. I think I knew you wouldn't laugh. I've always thought there was something about you that made you more sensitive than most other people. Maybe it's the way you paint; maybe it's just the way you act. You know, sort of carefully, as if you don't want anyone to get hurt by what you do or say. You're very tuned in to other people. It's almost as if you have a sixth sense about how to make people feel at ease. People just know they can trust you."

What a lovely thing to say! Chris was flattered, until she realized that it was Susan that Keith was talking about, not her. In fact, she doubted that anyone would ever say something like that about her. Was it possible that worrying about what other people thought, at least in terms of being careful not to hurt their feelings, was a good thing? Chris vowed to start being more sensitive to people. From now on, she would take the time to think about how people might react to some of the more outrageous things she said.

"Here we are!" Keith jumped up and started for the door of the bus. For a split second Chris thought he was going to take her hand. She wished he would, but he was still basically shy, no matter how honest he was being with her. As they crossed the street to the skating rink, she was tempted to take his arm. But she held herself back, not wanting to make him ill at ease.

Keith seemed to like quiet girls, something that had never even occurred to Chris before. She just assumed boys liked their dates to be talkative and clever, constantly joking and teasing them. Was Keith really that different? Or had she been acting too flippant all along?

Maybe that was why Chris's dates never asked her out more than two or three times. Perhaps they got tired of her lack of seriousness after a while. Now, that was something to think about.

The rest of the evening proceeded like a dream. Keith was the perfect date as far as Chris was concerned. He was considerate, constantly asking her if she was thirsty, if she was tired of skating, if she was cold and wanted to wear his sweater.

They spent almost two hours skating. Keith was a good skater, and the two of them developed a kind of routine that enabled them to circle the ring together without falling or getting in each other's way. When Chris was skating alone and two or three boys asked her to skate with them, she had no qualms about telling them no, that she was there with someone. In the past she had found many of her dates boring, and she had been all too willing to switch dance partners or bowling partners, hoping to find someone more interesting. But for some reason, spending time with Keith was so much fun that she didn't want to waste any time with any other boys, even those who were better-looking or older or more outgoing.

When they both agreed that they felt as if their feet were going to fall off, Chris and Keith returned their skates to the rental office and walked down the street to an area filled with fast-food places and small restaurants.

"I don't know about you," said Keith, "but I'm starving. All that exercise really wore me out. I have a feeling I won't be able to walk tomorrow!"

"Me, too! Not only are my muscles starting to yell at me, asking me what in the world I've done to them; I'm also tired mentally from all that concentrating. When you have to keep thinking about what you're doing so you don't fall, it's as draining as taking an exam at school!"

"Well, milady, you have your choice of hot spots. What kind of food are you in the mood for?"

"How about a hamburger? I'm about ready for a second dinner!"

"You've got great taste, Susan. I could really go for a sloppy hamburger, with millions of french fries and a whole vatful of Coke. And then, for the main course . . ."

"Oh, you!" Chris teased, punching him playfully in the arm. She froze then, realizing that that was a very Chris thing to do. But Keith didn't seem to mind. In fact, once she had broken the ice by touching him in such a natural, joking way, she felt that much closer to Keith. He apparently felt it, too, for he reached over and took her hand. Chris had held hands with a lot of boys in her day, but never had it been as sweet as this. She could tell that Keith didn't have too much experience going out with girls. So the simple, innocent act of taking her hand was much more meaningful to him than it was to most of the boys she went out with, and that made it mean more to her, too.

While they gorged themselves on a snack just like the one Keith had described, Chris and he kidded each other about the way they skated. But then the conversation became much more serious, with Keith telling her more about why he wanted to be a doctor and how much it meant to him. Again Chris was struck by the contrast between him and her usual dates. Usually she plastered an interested look on her face and let the boy she was out with talk all he wanted while she daydreamed or kept her eyes open to see who else came into the restaurant.

But she was genuinely fascinated by what Keith had to say. Maybe it was because he was a deeper person; maybe it was just because she liked him so much. At any rate, she was so busy asking him questions and listening to him that she had little time to say much about herself. Or rather, about Susan.

"Gee, look at the time!" Keith exclaimed when only a few soggy french fries were left and all the ice in the paper cups had melted. "I'd better get you home, or your father will never let me take you out again!"

Chris was pleased. But then she remembered the awful truth. It was possible that she would have the chance to go out with Keith one more time, the following weekend, which was the last two days of the Banana Split Affair. But after that it would be Susan, not she, who got to date him. Her sister would go skating with him and share french fries with him and talk to him for hours. The real Susan would be the one to hold his hand and, eventually, to kiss him. It wasn't fair! Chris found herself hating the Banana Split Affair. If it weren't for their stupid game, she never would have met Keith! Not unless he became Susan's boyfriend. And then she would never have had the chance to find out what a really special guy he was!

Chris was quiet as she and Keith sat in the back of the bus, riding toward her house.

"Is there anything wrong, Susan? Or are you just tired? It is awfully late. . . ."

"What? Oh, I'm sorry. I guess I was just daydreaming."

"About what?"

Chris glanced over at him, then blushed beet red. "Well, about tonight, as a matter of fact."

"Really? What were you thinking?" He grabbed her purse out of her lap and said teasingly, "Come on, Susan. If you don't tell me, I'll steal your pocketbook. I'll throw it into the river. Or better yet, I'll have it bronzed. . . ."

Chris laughed. "It's kind of embarrassing, that's all. To tell you the truth," she said with a slight hesitation, "I was daydreaming about you."

"About me? Why daydream about me when you've got the real thing right here, sitting next to you?" More seriously, he said, "No, really, Susan, you don't have to tell me. I have no right to pry into your thoughts. Of course, now that you've told me you were daydreaming about *me*, I'm dying to know . . ."

"Well," Chris sighed, without looking at him. "I was thinking about how nice it would be to go out with you again. That's all."

"And here I was expecting you to say you were thinking that my ears were too big or my feet reminded you of turnips or something horrible like that!" He chuckled. "But really, Susan, I think that's nice that you told me. Especially since I've been thinking the same thing all evening. I hope we can keep going out for a long time. I really like you. And I'm not afraid to admit it, the way some people are. I hope we can spend a lot of time together. I had a really terrific time tonight."

"Thanks, Keith. I'm glad you're being so honest, too." She smiled at him sadly. This was even worse! Not only did she like him a lot; he felt the same way about her! That meant that he and Susan would continue going out, probably for a long, long time, and she would just sit by and watch! How would she be able to stand it? And she would never be able to breathe a word of the truth about her feelings to her twin, either. She would have to live with this secret forever. Why, oh, why did I ever agree to go through with this? she asked herself again. I never suspected I would end up getting so hurt!

The bus ride was over too soon, and Keith and Chris jumped off a block from her house. As they walked down the street together hand in hand, Chris thought, I know what I'll do. I won't kiss him good-night. That way, once I become Chris again and I can't go out with him anymore, I won't feel quite as bad.

But when Keith walked her up to the front steps and looked at her with that watery expression in his eyes that said he was about to kiss her, she eagerly leaned forward to meet his lips. She expected to feel guilty kissing him, but all she was aware of was how nice it felt to be so close to him.

"Good night, Susan," he said softly. "I'll see you in class on Monday. That is, if I can manage to wait that long."

"Good night, Keith." She was torn between feeling the thrill of coming home after a wonderful evening and the sadness of inevitable separation. "And thanks for a terrific time."

She waited until he had disappeared into the night,

then let herself into the house. Her parents were in the living room, watching the news.

"Hi!" she said with forced cheerfulness, strolling in.

"Hello, whoever you are," returned her father. "You're home right on time, I'm happy to see. Did you have a good time?"

Chris just shrugged. "Okay, I guess. But I'm bushed. Think I'll go right up to bed. Good night!"

"That must be Susan," she heard her mother comment as she went up the stairs to her room. "If it were Chris, she would insist upon giving us a rundown of how terrific her evening was and how wonderful the boy she went out with is."

If you only knew, she thought, going into her bedroom and closing the door behind her. My evening was so terrific, and the boy I went out with so wonderful, that to talk about it would spoil it. And make it hurt that much more later on.

"Well, Chris," she said aloud, kicking off her shoes and pulling out the tortoiseshell barrette she had clipped into her hair for the evening, "you're back to being yourself again. Miss Popularity. Hah!"

Never before had her role as one of the best-known, best-liked girls at school seemed so ironic. Chris had always prided herself on her active social life, her outstanding popularity. But now she found herself hating that distinction.

"Chris Pratt," she mumbled, climbing into her nightgown and sliding into bed, "famous for being the girl who can get any boy she wants.

"Any boy, that is, except for the one she wants most!"

Thirteen

Susan stood in front of the telephone, staring at it as if it were some strange thing she had never seen before. She picked up the receiver, then quickly dropped it. It was the tenth time she had tried to make her phone call. But every time she got ready to do it, she got scared and hung up.

"*Call him!*" Chris had advised her after she poured out her sad story of her date with Jason Simms. "Look, you two only went out together once. You need more time than that to find out if you like someone or not. Besides, you were so busy trying to act like me—or the way you thought I would act—that you never even got the chance to find out if you have anything in common or not."

"What if he hangs up on me?" Susan protested. "He made it sound as if he never wanted to see me again. I made such a fool of myself that I can hardly blame him. But I don't want to make things even worse by having him refuse to talk to me on the phone!"

"Come on, Sooz. If this guy is as nice and as reasonable as you claim he is, he'll at least hear you out."

"But what should I say?"

"Hmmm. According to the contract of the Banana Split Affair, you're not allowed to tell him that you're really someone else. And we agreed that you'd act like me no matter what. But what you *can* do is apologize for your behavior and say that the reason you were acting so strange was that you were nervous. And then . . ."

"Yes?"

"And then ask him out."

"What?" Susan shrieked.

"You heard me perfectly well. I said, Ask him out. Girls call boys and ask them for dates all the time. After all, it *is* the 1980s, not the 1950s. Where have you been, twin?"

"I know that, of course. But Jason . . . Jason *hates* me! Why would he possibly agree to go out with me again?"

"Because," Chris had explained patiently, "you will have explained that the person he went out with Saturday night was not the real you. That you want a second chance so that he can see who the real you is."

"What if he says no? Or gets mad? Or, worse yet, laughs at me?"

"Look, Sooz. If he reacts that way, then we'll both know what kind of guy he is, that he's not worth wasting time on. But if he's halfway decent, he'll accept your apology and agree to give it another try."

Finally Chris had managed to convince her more retiring twin that she had absolutely nothing to lose by calling Jason. So Susan stood in front of the telephone for almost fifteen minutes, trying to muster up the courage to dial his number.

As she timidly reached for the receiver one more time, she heard Chris call to her from her bedroom, "Call him! Call him already! It's a rainy Sunday afternoon, the best time to find someone in. If you don't call, *I* will!"

"Okay, okay," Susan called back. She picked up the receiver and this time dialed Jason's number.

Maybe he won't be home, she thought. Maybe he left town.

Then she heard his voice. "Hello?"

"Hello, Jason?" Her throat suddenly got dry, and her stomach started to ache.

"Yes, speaking. Who is this, please?"

"Uh, this is Chris Pratt."

After a painful silence that seemed to last forever, he cleared his throat and said, "Oh, hi, Chris. How are you?"

"I'm fine, Jason. Listen, I feel kind of strange calling you like this, especially since things didn't go too well last night."

"I wouldn't say . . ."

"Please listen, Jason. I know I acted really stupid last night. I said a lot of dumb things. But I want you to know that I'm not really like that. Not at all. I was very nervous, that's all. I was trying too hard to impress you. And so everything came out all wrong. I could tell as soon as I said anything that I sounded ridiculous. But for some reason, I kept right on talking. Even *I* didn't recognize myself!"

"Well, gee, Chris, I don't know what to say. It's just that you seemed so different last night from the way you were when we first met. Of course, I was pretty flustered

that day, but still, I didn't remember you being so . . .
so . . ."

"So smart-alecky." Susan supplied the word for him.
"I hope you understand, Jason. I'm not usually so hard
to get along with. And I was hoping that maybe you
would agree to, uh . . ."

"Yes, Chris?"

"Well, there's a basketball game at my high school
Wednesday night. I was wondering if you'd like to go."

That had been Chris's idea. "Boys love basketball,"
she had insisted. "And you won't have to worry about
making conversation for hours on end. Besides, since
you'll be going out on a weekday, you'll both have to get
home early. It should be nice and informal, with very
little pressure. Try it!"

"Well, sure, Chris. That sounds like fun."

Susan breathed a sigh of relief that was so loud she
was certain that Jason heard it. "Great! It starts at
eight. . . ."

"Fine. I'll borrow my father's car again and pick you
up at seven-thirty."

"Okay. See you then." Susan hung up the phone, then
yelled, "I did it! I did it!" She skipped into her sister's
bedroom.

"And? What did he say?"

"Why, he said yes, of course." Susan grinned at her
sister. "Did you ever have any doubts that he would?"

With that, Chris threw a pillow at her. "I hate to say I
told you so, but I told you so!"

Susan's second date with Jason proceeded much more
smoothly. She was careful not to make any more
outrageous remarks. Instead she filled Jason in on as
much as she knew about her school's basketball team.

Then, during the game, there was hardly any time at all for conversation except during halftime. And then Susan proudly introduced Jason to as many of Chris's friends as she could. She was in a wonderful mood; she was even able to spare a smile and a friendly wave for Richard Collier, whom she spotted standing by the refreshment stand over in the corner of the gym.

The game was over by ten, with the home team's four-point lead giving them another victory. Everyone's spirits were high, including Susan's and Jason's.

"That was an exciting game!" Jason exclaimed as he and Susan followed the crowd to the school parking lot. "I had no idea your school had such a good team! It was almost as much fun as watching a pro team."

"Yes, they are pretty good," Susan agreed. In truth she had only been to three or four games in her entire life, and she had had difficulty following it.

"Are you hungry?" Jason asked. "Would you like to go out for something to eat?"

"I'd love to. Unless, of course, you have to return your father's car early tonight, as well."

She had meant for her comment to be a joke. After all, she had known full well that Jason had merely been looking for an excuse to escape from their deadly date Saturday night when he made up that lie. Even so, he cast one of his bewildered glances in her direction.

Here I go again! Susan thought, biting her lip. Saying the wrong thing again. I thought I'd learned my lesson!

"No, we have time," Jason answered quietly.

Susan suggested they try an ice cream parlor nearby that was popular with the kids in her school, especially after games. The high spirits of her schoolmates would make it more exciting than any hamburger place.

Susan and Jason found a free table in the back, far

enough away from the boisterous crowd that they could hear each other talk. They were there to get to know each other, not to celebrate the school team's victory.

"That's quite a rowdy bunch," Jason commented after he had ordered a Chocolate Nut Supreme and Susan had asked for a Hot Butterscotch Sundae. "Are you friends with those kids?"

Susan surveyed the crowd. Sure enough, many of the kids who were playing the jukebox and dancing and talking and screaming at the top of their lungs were Chris's friends. She even recognized some of them from the party at Slade's a few nights before.

"Yes, as a matter of fact, I am," she replied. "Those are the important kids at school, for the most part."

" 'Important?' What do you mean by that?"

"Oh, you know. Student government officers, team captains, cheerleaders . . . like that. Important."

"Oh." Jason was wearing a strange smile. "It seems funny that you would use the word 'important' to describe people like that."

"Why?" That was the word Chris always used, wasn't it?

"Because they're not really any more 'important' than any other student in your school. They may be more active or more visible or even more popular . . ."

"You know what I mean. Those are the kids that count. The kids that everyone knows."

Jason shook his head slowly. "Yes, Chris, I know what you mean. I'm just saying that it's kind of strange that you think of them that way. It's almost as if they were better than everybody else, just because they have a lot of dates and go to a lot of meetings after school."

Susan was dumbfounded. She was glad that their waitress arrived just then, bringing two heaping ice cream concoctions to distract them. Nothing more was said about either Chris's friends or the words that were commonly used to describe them.

Susan and Jason slurped up their desserts with so much concentration that there was little time for conversation. When they finally finished, Susan leaned back in her seat and said, in her most Christine-like manner, "Boy, I bet there were about nine thousand calories in that. I can feel myself growing fat right before your eyes."

"Boy," Jason said between spoonfuls of melted ice cream, "you sure know how to ruin something good." He glanced up at her immediately. "Hey, I'm sorry, Chris. I didn't mean that. Really. It just bugs me when a girl starts talking about how guilty she feels about eating something fattening when I'm out with her. Especially when she's thin, like you are. For heaven's sake, if you don't want it, don't eat it. But don't try to make everybody else feel bad for eating it by pointing out how bad it is for you."

Susan blanched. She had done it again. Whenever she tried to be true to the Banana Split pact and act like Chris, she made Jason drift further and further away. And she liked him so much! It wasn't fair: The more time they spent together, the more she liked him. And the more *he* disliked *her*!

"Are you finished, Chris?"

Susan nodded.

"I guess we should get going," he said, glancing at his watch. "But there's something I'd like to say first."

"Sure, Jason. What is it?"

"This isn't easy, Chris, but there's no use in pretending. Look. You're a nice girl and all, but I just don't think you and I were cut out for each other. We've gone out twice now, and it seems that every time I start to relax and have fun, you make some crazy remark that ruins everything! I don't think there's much use in us going out together anymore."

"Okay," Susan said softly. "If that's what you've decided." She stared at the empty dish of ice cream that sat in front of her, unwilling to look him in the eye.

"You see, Chris, the kind of girl I usually go for is much quieter than you. You know the type. Some people consider them bookworms, or eggheads. I'm not much for school politics or hanging around with a bunch of kids who spend more time getting drunk and dancing and having a good time than reading or thinking or planning where they want to go in life. Not that there's anything wrong with being like that. Sometimes I wish I could be looser and more fun-loving. But I'm kind of an egghead, too. The kind of kid that your friends usually make fun of. I'm afraid you and I don't have much in common," he finished.

If only he knew! Susan thought. If only I could tell him! The girl he's describing is me, the real me! The other one, the Chris one, is only a part I'm playing. I wish I could explain! Oh, I hate this stupid Banana Split agreement.

"Jason," she said cautiously, "I hear what you're saying about you and Christine Pratt being very different. And you're absolutely right. But let me ask you one thing. Do you think you could give me one more chance? I know you don't understand why, but believe me, there is a reason. A very good reason. Could we try this again next week?"

"I don't know, Chris. I don't think it's worth . . ."

"*Please*, Jason. You've got to trust me. You have to give me this one more chance."

Jason sighed and shrugged his shoulders. "I thought I explained things pretty clearly, Chris. I don't see why you have to make it even harder. You and I are just not right for each other."

"I know we're not. You're completely right. I'm not disagreeing with you. I just want a chance to explain. . . . Just say yes. Even for half an hour?"

"Well, okay. Since it's so important to you. Although I really don't understand why."

"Oh, thanks, Jason. Believe me. It'll make sense later on. I can't tell you any more, but trust me. I have my reasons."

"Okay."

Susan felt hopeful as she and Jason put on their coats and started for the car.

"Oh, by the way," he said offhandedly as they slid out the front door of the ice cream parlor, "the date for the hearing has been set. It's at the end of next week. You should be receiving notification any day now."

A shiver ran down Susan's spine. She had almost forgotten all about the hearing and the accident and the fact that she had lied about her true identity. The hearing would take place after the Banana Split Affair was over, but she would still have to explain why she had lied to the policeman. Was that a very bad offense, she wondered? Was lying to an officer a crime? There was no one she dared ask, not even Chris. She felt dizzy with fear. She was quiet as Jason drove her home, but her silence had nothing to do with role playing. She was numb with anxiety.

What now? she thought as she watched trees and houses pass by, dark and shadowy and slightly menacing. I may be able to win Jason back once I tell him the truth about the prank my twin and I are playing. But what about the courts? How will I ever explain why I lied?

By the time Jason took her home and walked her up to the front door, she was so jittery that she just wanted to get away from him and be alone. Before, she had wondered if he would kiss her good-night or at least say something pleasant about their evening together. But now she just muttered. "Good night," and ran inside the house.

Peculiar girl, thought Jason, shaking his head as he walked back to his car. It's almost as if she's so mixed up she doesn't even know who she is. I'll never be able to figure that one out!

Even so, as he drove home alone, he found that there was something about Chris Pratt that nagged at him. He wanted to forget all about her and her strange behavior, but he couldn't.

This has turned into kind of a mystery, he mused. And I'm not going to give up on Chris until I find out what's going on!

Fourteen

"Well, we made it."

The twins were in Susan's room, studying the big calendar with art reproductions printed on it. It was Saturday evening, the last night before the Banana Split Affair officially ended. But instead of sounding gleeful or even sad, Chris merely sounded tired.

"Yeah, we really did," Susan agreed in the same somber tone. "I never thought we'd be able to get through the whole two weeks, but we did. And not one single person guessed that we had switched identities."

"So now you owe me a banana split."

"Yeah. I know."

There was a long, mournful silence. It was Chris who finally broke it.

"Sooz, what's wrong with us? We should be feeling *something*. Victorious, because we managed to fool everybody. Or we should feel bad because the game is over and now it's time to go back to normal life. Or at least pleased that now we can go out and gorge ourselves on banana splits. I mean according to our agreement, mine is even *free*, since you'll be paying for it."

"I know," Susan sighed. "So what's wrong with us? Why are we reacting . . . by not reacting at all?"

Although Chris would never dare admit it to her sister, she knew exactly why she was acting so serious. As of tomorrow, when she turned back into Chris Pratt once again, she would never be able to go out with Keith West again. After all the boys she had gone out with, after the countless dates she had gone on, she had finally found the perfect boy for her. She had even gone so far as to fall in love with him. At least, she thought she was in love with Keith. Having never been in love before or felt anything stronger than mild infatuation, she couldn't be sure. All she knew was that Keith West made her feel better about herself and the world and just being alive than anybody else she had ever met.

And now not only would she have to give him up; she would have to stand by silently and watch her twin sister go out with him. Every Saturday night *Susan* would be humming as she got ready to go out with Keith. *Susan* would be the one to come home from a date with him, glowing and smiling. *She* would be the one to share inside jokes with him, receive sentimental valentine cards from him, sit in dark movie theaters and hold hands with him. Meanwhile, Chris would have to carry around the secret that she was actually jealous of her own twin. It wasn't fair!

Susan, on the other hand, was scared. There were two things plaguing her. One was that she had only one more chance to go out with Jason and try to show him what she was really like. That would be after the Banana Split Affair was over and she could go back to being herself. The second thing bothering her, the one that *really* frightened her, was the fact that the hearing for the car accident was only a few days away.

As both sisters stared at the calendar, they were both thinking the very same thing: Why, on why, did we ever get tangled up in this mess? If only we had been content to be ourselves, without fooling around with each other's identities!

"It's seven-thirty," Chris finally said. "I guess I should start getting ready for my date with Keith." My *last* date, she thought grimly.

"Yes," Susan agreed, "it *is* getting late. Just think: After tomorrow, I'll be the one going out with Keith." Even though I no longer have an interest in him at all, except as a friend and fellow art student. If only I could trade him for Jason! But poor Keith thinks he's been going out with me, Susan, all along. I can't just drop him without any explanation at all. I'll have to try to forget Jason and go back to liking Keith. As if it's possible to turn your affections on and off like a faucet!

Chris dragged herself off the floor, where she had been sitting cross-legged. "Here I go. I was going to wash my hair, but I don't have time now."

"You look like you dread going," Susan remarked. "Is Keith really that bad?"

"Oh, no. Of course not. I'm just in a funny kind of mood tonight. Maybe because it's the end of the Banana Split Affair."

"Maybe."

"What are you going to do tonight, Susan? After all, this is your last night as Chris Pratt."

"Nothing much. Just stay home, maybe do some homework. I'll probably go to bed early. I'm bushed, for some reason. Must be the strain of the last two weeks."

"Well, have a good time."

"Yeah," Susan said dully. "You, too."

Both girls went about their business—Chris back to her room to change her clothes, Susan back to her worrying—with the same reluctant attitudes. Neither of them could believe that something that had started out as such a lark had ended so miserably.

"This *was* supposed to be a learning situation," Susan told herself, staring at the ceiling as she lay back on her bed to think. "But why is the best way to learn things always the hardest, most painful way?"

A few hours later Chris came up the stairs quietly, careful not to wake her sister. It was late, and she had missed her curfew by over an hour. But she didn't care, not this time. She would rather get yelled at by her parents or even be grounded than cut short her final date with Keith. Her final date. That thought had buzzed around in her mind the whole evening. The more fun she was having with him, the worse she felt. Not only because she would never go out with him again, either. She felt she was betraying her sister by enjoying Keith's company, holding hands with him, flirting, and even kissing him. What a confusing situation she had gotten herself into!

As she tiptoed past her twin's bedroom door, she was surprised to see a light peeking out underneath. Was Susan still awake? Even though she had planned to turn in early? She knocked on the door softly.

"Chris? Is that you? Come on in. I've been waiting up for you."

Chris opened the door and went in. Her sister was sitting in bed with the covers pulled up to her chin, wearing a miserable expression on her face.

"Susan! Are you okay? You look terrible!"

"Chris, I have to talk to you. You're probably going to think I'm ridiculous and stupid afterward, but there's something I have to tell you. I have to tell *somebody*, or I'll go crazy. And you're the only person in the world who could possibly understand."

"What is it?" Chris sat down gingerly on the edge of her sister's bed, as if she were visiting a sick person who couldn't be jostled.

"Oh, Chris, I've done something terrible. You know Jason, don't you?"

"You've told me about him. But I've never met him. Neither have Mom and Dad, come to think of it. Have you been hiding him from us for some reason?"

"Yes, I have. But it has nothing to do with him. Do you have any idea how I met him?"

"Didn't you say he was the friend of one of your girl friends?"

"That's what I told you, but that's not the truth. When I was walking home from school one day, I was the only witness to a car accident. Jason's car was hit by a man who ran a stop sign."

"What's wrong with that? I don't understand why that's such a big secret."

"Oh, Chris! When the policeman asked me my name, since I was the only witness and would probably be called upon to testify at a hearing, I gave *your* name!"

"*My* name! What for?"

"Because we were in the middle of the Banana Split Affair, and I didn't know what else to do! I remembered our pact, that we were supposed to switch identities no matter what. I couldn't think straight, and all of a sudden I just blurted out your name. I regretted it immediately, but it was already too late."

"Oh, dear. And there really is going to be a hearing?"

Susan nodded. There were tears in her eyes. "There's another part, too, although it's not nearly as bad. I like Jason a lot. A *real* lot, Chris. More than any boy I've ever met. But I kept pretending I was you. And I kept acting horrible, saying stupid, brash things. . . ."

"Thanks a lot!"

"Well, boys always seem to love it when you tease them. That's all I was trying to do."

"Yes, but there's a certain art to it. Besides, I'm beginning to see myself that maybe it's not such a good idea to be a flirt all the time. People begin to think you're empty-headed if you're never serious."

"I know exactly what you mean. Anyway, Jason told me right out that he didn't like girls like that. He prefers quiet girls, the way I *really* am! When he said that, I asked him for one more chance. We're going out next week sometime, when I'm back to being Susan. But I'm afraid it might be too late."

"Maybe you could explain the Banana Split Affair to him," Chris suggested.

"Not on your life! Then he'd really think I was insincere! If he finds out I wasn't even acting like myself, that even my *name* was false, he'd never forgive me!"

Chris sighed. "It might be worth a try, though. You have nothing to lose."

"I suppose," Susan said thoughtfully.

Chris took a deep breath. "Hey, Sooz, since you've been so honest with me, I'm afraid there's something I have to tell you, too. You might end up hating me for the rest of your life, but I have to tell you. I can't go on keeping secrets from you forever."

"What is it?"

"Rather than beat around the bush, I might as well tell

you straight out. Susan, I think I've fallen in love with Keith West."

Susan's mouth dropped open.

"Now wait. Before you say anything, let me explain. When I first started talking to him, I was thinking only of you. I mean, you did ask me to try to catch his attention while I was pretending I was you, right? I considered it my sisterly duty. But the more I talked to him, the more I grew to like him. And then when I started going out with him, I discovered I could talk to him, and be myself, in a way I never could before with any other boy. It was exhilarating, you know? Except the whole time I kept thinking about you and how I was betraying you. It was *you* he was supposed to like. And there I was, acting as if he and I were a couple. Oh, Susan, I feel just awful. Can you ever forgive me?"

Instead of frowning or breaking into tears the way Chris expected, her twin sister started to laugh. She leaned forward and threw her arms around her.

"Oh, Christine! My dear, sweet twin! Don't you understand? I'm *glad* you like Keith! As a matter of fact, I'm *thrilled*! Don't you know how infatuated I am with Jason? I have no interest in Keith anymore! I'm positively *relieved* that I don't have to pretend to like him after tomorrow and keep going out with him simply because he likes *you* so much!"

"Well, that's a relief!"

"Of course! I much prefer Jason. With all due respect to Keith, he just doesn't compare, as far as I'm concerned! Of course," she added quickly, "if you want to go out with him, I'm sure he's terrific."

"He is." Chris laughed. "And you don't have to pretend you think so. In fact, I'd like it better if you didn't think he was so hot! After being jealous of you for the past two weeks, it'd make my life a lot easier if I was sure you had completely forgotten about him."

"Well, that's all settled!" Susan exclaimed. "Now there's only one minor problem."

"What's that?"

"How are we going to manage to switch back to our real identities without having Jason and Keith notice that something strange is going on?"

"You're right," Chris groaned. "We can't. Once you're Susan again, it won't take him long to figure out that the girl in his art class is not the same one he takes to the movies that night! We can't go on pretending forever."

"I know. And then there's Jason. I have only one date to convince him that I really am the kind of girl he likes. You know, the egghead type."

There was a long silence as both girls thought about their dilemma.

"You realize, of course," Chris finally said, "that there's only one thing for us to do."

"I know. We have to tell both boys about the Banana Split Affair. There's no other way to get around it."

"They'll never understand." Chris frowned. "Never. Keith will feel he's been tricked."

"So will Jason. But I guess we have no other choice. We've gotten ourselves into this mess, and now we have to try to talk our way out of it."

"I'm not looking forward to this. That's for sure."

"Look, Chris. It's late. Why don't we sleep on it, and if we still think it's what we have to do tomorrow morning, we can call the boys and arrange a double date. I think it'll be easier if we have each other there for moral support."

"That's a good idea," Chris agreed.

"You know, Jason doesn't even know I have a twin sister. He'll be flabbergasted when he meets you!"

"I don't think Keith realizes there are two of us either. That school of ours is so big that he's probably never even seen me."

"In that case, both boys are in for a *really* big surprise. Double trouble."

"Are you referring to *us* as 'double trouble,' my dear twin?" Chris joked.

"Well, we are, aren't we?"

"Let's just hope Keith and Jason don't think so. They'd better have a good sense of humor, or we'll both become wallflowers. Very unhappy wallflowers, too."

"Don't even think that way. Be positive." Susan glanced over at the clock on her night table. "It's late, Chris. We'd better get some sleep. Tomorrow is going to be a big day for both of us."

"For all four of us, you mean." Chris stood up to leave. "I'll say good night, but I don't think I'll get much sleep tonight."

"Me either. But just think: If we can all get together tomorrow, everything will be resolved, one way or the other, by tomorrow night at this time."

"Right. 'One way or the other.' Somehow I'm not exactly thrilled with those odds!"

"Go to sleep!" Susan insisted, pulling the covers over her head. "We need our rest for the big confrontation tomorrow."

Confrontation, thought Chris as she tossed and turned, trying to unwind. What a frightening word! It was a long, long time before she finally fell asleep.

Fifteen

Chris and Susan sat opposite each other in a red vinyl booth at a local coffee shop on Sunday afternoon, trying to make small talk. But the fact that both of them were scared stiff was obvious. They had taken back their own identities, and oddly enough, it was taking them some time to get used to being themselves again.

"What time is it?" Chris asked, drumming on the table nervously.

"Christine," Susan said crossly, "that's the twentieth time you've asked me that in the past ten minutes. It's five minutes after two." She twisted a strand of hair around her finger.

"Where are they? Do you think maybe they're not coming?"

"I know Jason's coming. He's promised to give me one more chance. I told him he didn't have to spend any more than fifteen minutes with me if he didn't want to but that he at least had to hear me out. I'm positive he'll be here." She glanced over at the glass door of the restaurant, hoping to see his familiar outline, but there was no one there except a father who had just bought ice cream cones for his three children.

"There's no reason why Keith shouldn't come. He thinks we're just getting together for a cup of coffee. Although I did mention that I had something in particular that I wanted to discuss with him."

"Oh, Chris, are you sure we're doing the right thing?"

"We've already been through this. We're doing the only thing we *can* do." Susan leaned her head in her hands. "I wish I'd never even heard of the Banana Split Affair."

"I know what you mean," Chris agreed. "I'll never be able to eat another banana split for the rest of my life." She twisted around in her seat so that she, too, could see the front door of the coffee shop. "I'm going crazy just sitting here waiting. I'm going to go peek out the window and see if I see any familiar cars coming into the parking lot."

Just as she neared the front of the restaurant, Keith walked in, wearing a big grin.

"Hiya, kiddo! Sorry I'm late. But you know how unreliable those buses are. You can never predict how long it's going to take you to get from one place to another." He leaned over and gave her a kiss on the cheek.

"Hi, Keith," said Chris. "You seem like you're in an awfully good mood."

"As a matter of fact, I am."

"That's good."

"Why?" He glanced at her quizzically. "Oh, that's right. Didn't you mention something over the phone about something important you wanted to discuss with me?" He frowned. "Not bad news, I hope."

"No, nothing bad. Just . . . surprising."

"Gee, now I'm dying to know what's going on. Let's find a quiet little table for two and you can fill me in."

"I already have a table, over there, behind that post."

"Okay. Then let's go sit down."

"Wait a second, Keith. I . . . there's someone sitting with us. Someone I'd like you to meet."

"Okay."

"But you'd better brace yourself."

"It's not your long-lost husband or anything like that, is it?"

"No." Chris laughed despite her nervousness.

"In that case, how bad can this be?"

He strode off in the direction she had indicated. All of a sudden he stopped dead in his tracks.

"Oh, my gosh!" he cried, so loudly that everyone in the restaurant looked up to see what the commotion was about. "You're her! I mean there's two of her. Two of you."

"Hi," Susan said meekly. "You already know me, Keith. I'm Susan Pratt, the girl in your art class."

"*You're* Susan? Then who is . . ." He turned around and faced Chris, totally bewildered. "Then who are you?"

"I'm *Chris* Pratt, Susan's twin sister."

"Twins!" He just stood still for a few seconds, his mouth wide open. "So if you're Susan and you're her sister, then who have I been going out with for the last two weeks?"

"You've been going out with me, Keith," answered Chris. "But I've been pretending to be Susan."

"Pretending to be Susan? I'm sorry if I sound dense,

but would someone please tell me what's going on here?"

"It's really quite simple," Chris began patiently. "For as long as we can remember, Susan has wondered what it would be like to be me. And I wondered what it would be like to be her. Since we're identical twins and people can never tell the difference between us *anyway* . . ." She went on to explain the Banana Split Affair and how it had come about. When she finished, Keith looked at her in amazement and plopped down into the booth opposite Susan.

"I don't believe it! I mean of all the devious, sneaky . . ."

"But we weren't trying to be sneaky!" Susan protested. "We weren't trying to hurt anybody or anything like that. We just wanted to see how it was to be the other twin. You can't look exactly like someone else all your life and *not* wonder what their life is like! We just went ahead and traded identities so that we could find out."

"Are you really mad, Keith?" Chris asked softly, sitting down next to him. "I don't blame you, I guess, but do you think you could ever forgive . . ."

Just then she was interrupted by a boisterous voice. "Hi, there! Hiya, Susan. I'm sorry I couldn't get here . . ." Jason stopped midsentence. "What is this? There are two of you! Well, I'll be!"

"Hello, Jason," said Susan. "I'm glad you could come."

"Am I seeing double?"

"No," Susan said calmly. "Why don't you have a seat? It'll be easier for you to take the shock if you're sitting down."

"Uh-oh," Jason muttered. "This doesn't sound good."

"First of all," Susan began, "let me introduce everyone. This is Keith West, who goes to our school."

"Hello, Keith. Are you sure there aren't any more people in this restaurant who look just like you?"

"Nope." Keith laughed. "I'm an original."

"Now," said Susan, "I'm the girl you've been going out with. I told you my name was Chris, but really it's Susan. Chris here is my twin sister."

"So why were you using her name? Ever since the accident . . . Oh, yes, that reminds me. Everything's been cleared up out of court. You won't have to appear after all. That creep who ran into me finally confessed that it was his fault. The fact that I had an eyewitness was what did the trick, too."

"Thank goodness!" Chris and Susan exchanged relieved looks.

"But which one of you really *did* see the accident, then?"

Susan explained the Banana Split Affair to him, every detail from start to finish. She ended it up by saying, "That's why it was so important that you give me one more chance, Jason. I wanted to tell you what was going on. We were sworn to secrecy during the last two weeks. But now that you know everything," she went on, turning bright pink, "I thought maybe we could give it another try. Since we didn't hit it off too well when I was trying to act like Chris, maybe things will go better when I'm acting like myself."

"Amazing," Jason breathed, shaking his head. "You two are really something!"

"Something good or something bad?" Susan ventured timidly.

The two boys exchanged glances. "What do you say,

Keith? Should we be mad at these two little devils or should we let them off easy?"

"I don't know," Keith said slowly. "After all, they made real fools out of us. Here we both thought we were going out with girls we thought we knew pretty well, and it turns out we had no idea of their real identity. We didn't even know there were two of them!"

"Yes, I guess that is pretty lousy," Jason agreed. "They've been playing games with us. Toying with our affections, you know?"

"We have not!" Chris protested. "Keith, I never lied to you about anything but my name."

"And the fact that you were the same girl who'd been in my art class all semester. Don't forget that."

"Well, yes, that's true." Chris shifted in her seat, growing more and more agitated. "But everything else I ever said or did was completely sincere."

"Even when you held my hand?"

"Yes."

"Even when you agreed that you wanted to keep on seeing me for a long time?"

"Definitely."

"Even when you kissed me?"

"Oh, yes. Especially then."

"Well, Jason," Keith said, "I've heard all I need to hear. How about you?"

"Tell me, Chris. I mean Susan. I described the kind of girl I'm most compatible with, remember? The egghead type, someone just like me? What makes you think that Susan Pratt and I would get along together any better than Chris Pratt and I?"

"I can answer that one," interjected Chris. "My sister here is the original bookworm. She's read books whose *titles* most people can't even pronounce! And she knows all about music and theater and art. In fact, she's a terrific artist herself.''

"I can vouch for that," volunteered Keith. "The real Susan is in my art class, and she's the most talented student in the whole school."

"I still don't know," Jason said slowly.

The two girls sat in silence. "I know that things got out of hand. . . ." Susan began.

"Women," sighed Jason. "You can't live with 'em, and you can't live without 'em. I guess we just have to accept these merry pranksters for what they are."

"You're absolutely right, Jason. We men have no choice. Besides, I have to admit that I'm kind of stuck on the mystery girl who pretended she was Susan but has turned out to be Chris."

"I know exactly what you mean. I've always had a funny feeling about the Chris sister who turned out to be Susan. I knew there was something going on, that there was more than what appeared on the surface. And now that I know what happened, I'm kind of flattered that she went to all this trouble to explain things and get them all straightened out."

"Well, Jason," Keith said, "it looks like we've got ourselves a couple of girl friends. Good old cupid just won't leave us nice guys alone."

"You're right," agreed Jason. "Why fight it?" He reached for Susan's hand under the table.

"What a relief!" Susan said to her sister.

"See? I hate to say 'I told you so,' but . . ."

"Do you remember, Chris, when we first started the Banana Split Affair? We were trying to get Mom and Dad's permission, so we told them it would be an educational experience. I didn't believe it at the time, but I have to admit now that I sure did learn a lot!"

"Me, too!" agreed Chris. "All about the way people react to other people and how to try changing the things I never liked about myself too much . . ."

"And I also learned that there's no one else I'd rather be than me!"

"Me too!" A bit embarrassed, Chris added, "Although I realized that there are some things about you that I'd like to incorporate into my own personality. Things like taking myself and other people more seriously, learning to do something worthwhile, like your art . . ."

"And I found out how much I'd been missing by hiding behind my shyness all my life!"

"Hey, are you two going to gab all day? I'm getting hungry," Keith exclaimed with mock anger. "And here comes our waitress, just in time."

"Hi, kids," said a young woman in a fresh pink uniform. "I'm Carol, your waitress for today. What would you like?"

All four exchanged glances and diabolical smiles. And then four voices cried out, "Banana splits, of course!" then burst into hysterical laughter.

ABOUT THE AUTHOR

Cynthia Blair grew up on Long Island, earned her B.A. from Bryn Mawr College in Pennsylvania, and went on to get a M.S. in marketing from M.I.T. She worked as a marketing manager for food companies but now has abandoned the corporate life in order to write.

She lives on Long Island with her husband, Richard Smith, and their son Jesse.